CHOPSTICK

Books by
Sandra Byrd
FROM BETHANY HOUSE PUBLISHERS

Girl Talk
Chatting With Girls Like You
A Growing-Up Guide
The Inside-Out Beauty Book
Stuff 2 Do

FRIENDS FOR A SEASON
Island Girl
Chopstick
Red Velvet

THE HIDDEN DIARY
Cross My Heart
Make a Wish
Just Between Friends
Take a Bow
Pass It On
Change of Heart
Take a Chance
One Plus One

FRIENDS for a SEASON

CHOPSTICK

Sandra Byrd

BETHANYHOUSE

MINNEAPOLIS, MINNESOTA

Published by Bethany House Publishers
11400 Hampshire Avenue South
Bloomington, Minnesota 55438

Bethany House Publishers is a division of
Baker Publishing Group, Grand Rapids, Michigan.

Printed in the United States of America

Library of Congress Cataloging-in-Publication Data

Byrd, Sandra.
    Chopstick / by Sandra Byrd.
        p.   cm. — (Friends for a season)
    Summary: Told in the alternating voices of two thirteen-year-old girls who
learn real lessons about faith while competing against one another in a worship-
music contest offering a four-hundred-dollar prize.
    ISBN 0-7642-0021-6 (pbk.)
    [1. Competition (Psychology)—Fiction.   2. Music—Competitions—
Fiction.   3. Christian life—Fiction.]   I. Title.
    PZ7.B9898Cho   2005
    [Fic]—dc22   2005005868

For Elizabeth Byrd

A lover of music,
a caretaker of both pets and kids,
and a young woman seeking to glorify God.

SANDRA BYRD lives near Seattle with her husband, two children, and a tiny Havanese circus dog named Brie. Besides writing *Island Girl* and the other FRIENDS FOR A SEASON books, Sandra is the bestselling author of the SECRET SISTERS SERIES, THE HIDDEN DIARY SERIES, and the nonfiction book collection GIRLS LIKE YOU.

Learn more about Sandra and her books at *www.friendsforaseason.com.*

CHAPTER ONE
lewiston, idaho

paige

We ate Chinese food on Tuesday, the night before it all began. The fortune inside my cookie said, "Big changes are coming." Everyone else at the table was talking and slurping noodles or crunching lemon chicken. I don't believe in fortunes printed in a factory somewhere in California by people as ordinary as myself, of course. But I slipped it into my pocket and then set it carefully on my dresser when I got home.

I wanted change so much.

As usual, Wednesday was a really busy day, even though we'd been in school for less than a month. English literature's allergic Miss Jones sniffed every thirty seconds instead of blowing her nose, Walter glued himself to my locker talking about his latest soccer score, and then after school yearbook met right up until it was time for Janie to pick me up. I'd brought a PowerBar to chow down on the way to church. No time for dinner on Wednesdays.

Wednesday evening was youth group. Janie went early, which of course meant I did, too—though today I'd want to anyway. People thought it was great that my older brother and sister could drive me places instead of my parents. In some ways it was better—the music in the car, for example, wasn't that easy listening doo-da. Janie and Justin usually didn't remember me in the backseat, so they'd talk about really interesting stuff. Afterward they'd stand around yakking with their mob, and I pretty much sat there by myself doodling in a notebook, pretending it didn't matter that no one was talking with me.

That was about to change.

Today was The Tryout.

As I waited for Janie, my backpack felt really heavy. It was stuffed with my music notebooks—all the music I'd written my whole life. I didn't know if they'd be interested in hearing any of my music or what. When you attend a big church, people don't know you right away. Since the junior high youth group was for seventh and eighth graders, you'd think they'd have had all of last year to get to know me, but apparently not. So here I was in eighth grade. They'd want to see what I could do. It was okay. I'd prove myself.

Janie's car rattled into the Whitewater Middle School parking lot to pick me up. I mean, there was something totally loose under the hood. Not that I'm complaining. In fact, the car will probably be mine someday. After Justin. Janie was going to college in ten months and two days. She'd told me again that morning. *Believe me,* I'd told her, *we're both counting the days.*

Justin would get a ride to church after football practice. I'd noticed he'd been packing gel in his duffel bag. Who was *he* expecting to see at youth group? He sure wasn't slicking back his hair for Janie and me. Actually, it looked a little goofy, like some of the singers on the doo-da station, but no one asked me.

"Meet me out here right away, okay?" Janie said when we got to church and she headed down the hall to the high school session. "I'm swamped with work and have to get home."

Did I forget to tell her I was trying out for the junior

high praise team, or did she just forget to wish me good luck?

I stepped into the room. Ever notice how you can tell how you're ranked by what happens in the room when you step into it? If you're a total popular, everyone stops talking. Then girls call out and come running over to you. They paw your clothes and your hair and say how great you look and then drag you over to where their chairs are circled in a powwow.

That didn't happen.

If you're a nerd, no one will even stop talking. In fact, it's like they know you're in the room by the vibe but don't bother to look at you. You glance around the room like a mouse when the light's flipped on.

That didn't happen, either.

If you're somewhere in between, the talking stops and a couple of people nod at you, then leave you to make your own way. But you still feel unwanted.

I made my way toward the front. The pastor's daughter, Mallory, was in charge of the team. Maybe if you have long blond hair cascading down your back like Rapunzel, you lead worship better. If you're the pastor's daughter you get privileges. Mallory's friend Britt stood guard in front of her. I wanted to feel bad for Britt because she was the anti-Rapunzel in every possible way, but she sure didn't make it easy.

"Hi," I said.

"Yeah?" Britt swung toward me.

"I'm here to try out for the spot on the praise team."

My friend Walter came into the room. The talking stopped in some corners, and there were some nods. Walter looked up at me. He set his guitar case down; he was the lead guitarist for our youth group. I smiled at him, hoping he'd come forward and tell this pack of girls how well I could sing and write music. Instead, he fiddled with his guitar strings in the back of the room. At least he didn't bring up soccer again.

"Have we met?" Mallory asked.

I nodded. "Are the tryouts for the praise team today?" I asked.

"They are," Britt said. "What exactly do *you* do?"

"I write music," I said. "I sing. I play keyboard."

"Write music? We're not cutting any CDs." She looked around to make sure her group giggled. Obediently, they did. "And we already have a keyboardist. Well, he's here sometimes, and sometimes he's not, but whenever he is here he's in charge," Britt said. "Do you play guitar?"

"Not yet. . . ." My voice trailed off.

"Do you sing lead?" Mallory asked. "I'm spending some time in the high school group, so we could use someone who sings lead." High school? She'd just started eighth grade, same as me.

"Yes." Honesty was the best policy, right? My grandma said it was. "I haven't done it a lot."

Mallory seemed nice in a chilly, princess-wave kind of way. I wanted to like her but didn't think I'd ever get close enough to try.

Mallory and Britt looked at each other. Walter came up to the stage that was set up at the front of the teen annex, and he pretty much nodded me toward the keyboard. My notebooks stayed hidden in my backpack.

"Do you know this one?" Mallory handed a sheet of music to me. Britt and some others talked in the corner of the room. The junior high pastor would be there soon, and I wanted to get going. If Rapunzel was going to kick me out of the tower, it'd go down easier in private.

I played the keyboard alone even though both of us were singing. The keys were comfortingly cool on my fingertips, and I disappeared into the music like I always did. When I resurfaced, the room had kind of quieted. The rest of the team were looking only at Mallory. I got that same creeping moss feeling I got when Janie and Justin forgot about me. Mallory smiled, and Britt came back over and rustled up a twisted grin before rushing Mallory off to the next group of people waiting to curtsy. "We'll call you tonight," she said.

"You sounded great," Walter said. "You're a genius on the keyboard."

"Thanks. Did you tell them?" I nodded hopefully toward the praise team.

"No, but I will, promise. Later, when stuff dies down," he said.

We studied Acts together in small groups. I really don't remember what we said or read or even prayed. I worried instead. I was too busy looking at the new girl sitting next to Mallory in her powwow. She'd tried out, too, after me. She hadn't seemed to play any instrument or sing lead, but maybe I hadn't noticed. I looked back at Mallory and doodled a poodle in my notebook.

Walter left as soon as youth group was over. He hadn't talked with Mallory or anyone. I tugged each of my cropped, low ponytails tighter and went to wait for Janie. She was already in the car. "Justin's riding home with some friends." She turned on the car, starting the rattle.

"I tried out tonight," I said, closing the passenger door. At least I could sit in the front. The soft leather hugged me, and I snuggled deeper into the seat.

"Oh, how'd it go?"

"I dunno."

"Paige, you always underestimate yourself. You probably did just fine." She reached into her purse and handed a stick of gum to me, and we drove with the music turned up while the wind jiggled the trees around us, mailing leaves from tree to street, where they landed like scattered letters in red and gold envelopes. I love getting mail. Even grade reports. Now that it was the end of September, I'd be getting the first one soon. I hoped my dad would notice.

When we got home, I went into the kitchen, where my mom was on the phone. She pointed toward the refrigerator and scratched something else into her Day-Timer. She must have learned short-hand in secretarial college or something, because I don't know how she fit it all in those little squares. I opened the fridge. There was a cheese and fruit plate, but it mostly had feta on it. Feta cheese smells like the inside of a belly button. No thanks. No Chinese leftovers. Even though I was starving, I just poured a bowl of cereal and went upstairs to my room.

Is there anything better than puppy love? My little dog, Brie, jumped up and down and rolled over and did tricks as soon as she saw me coming up the stairs.

"Hi, girl! Hi, Brie!" I rubbed her fuzzy tummy. Hey! Would my mom answer the phone if call waiting came through? They'd surely call within the hour. Right?

I went over to check on the other animals in my homemade animal foster home system. The hamster still had a gash on her left ear where another hamster had attacked her at the pet store. The people at the store had called and told me they'd give her to me for free if I could care for her. I took her, of course. They knew who to call. After all, who knows what would have been gashed next? I had a plan to place her in a loving home after she was well again. I sometimes baby-sat for this little girl who was the daughter of a friend of my mom's. After I promised her that hamsters don't stink and it's better if you have only one of them, she said she'd take her when the ear was healed. That little girl was lonely, too. They'd make a good pair. She'd love the hamster up good. She was already saving clothes from her Barbie collection to dress her up.

"Hey! No bullying!" One of my fish tried to keep the others away from the food. "I should flush you." I separated him into a tiny jelly jar instead. "That's how we deal with bullies." For a brief moment an image of Britt trapped in a tiny jelly jar came to mind. By sheer willpower, I banished it. At least I hadn't imagined her flushed.

It was eight-fifteen—was my mom off the phone yet? I ran downstairs to look. Nope. How long could it take them to call? She put her hand over the mouthpiece of the phone and whispered to me, "Hi, honey! Could you go get the mail?" She blew me a kiss, and I slipped on some socks and went to get the mail. I hate shoes but like socks. We buy them at

Goodwill so I can wear them out and not hear about it.

The driveway was cold; the chill from the asphalt seeped into my feet.

"Paige!" A voice crackled from the end of the driveway.

"Oh, hello, Mrs. Kellie. How are you?"

"Fine, thank you. Had my garden club today and then a potluck. Never a quiet moment."

I think she kept busy on purpose. Her husband died six months ago, and even though it was hard, she never let it beat her into the ground. She still got up every day and made her coffee and got her breakfast and wore nice grandma clothes like gray or black wool pants and sweater vests. She still did her makeup and went to Bible study. She waved to me as she got her mail and walked, with Kitty in her arms, back to her house. You never saw Mrs. Kellie without Kitty. They clung to each other in a sometimes lonely world.

I riffled through the mail as I walked to the house. Something for me from the pet shelter! Before I could open it, my mom stuck her head into the foyer. "You had a phone call. Someone named Walter."

Grr. She didn't even remember who my friends were. And why was Walter calling? I'd expected Mallory to call. Or Britt! But maybe that was good.

Maybe they had a friend call me to share the good news.

I ran upstairs, but Janie was on the telephone. "Get off!" I pounded on her door. So much for her load of homework.

While I waited, I brought up my email, as well as the youth worship site that I'd found after reading a notice stuck on the bulletin board in the lunchroom at my dad's office. Had anyone responded to my request?

Hey! Someone had responded. I could tell, because in the email subject line was "Guitar," and it had been sent only a minute or two ago!

"I'm off." Janie stuck her head into my bedroom. I turned around and grabbed the phone.

I made sure the door was tightly closed and called Walter.

"Hey, it's Paige. You called?"

"Yeah," he said. "Well, I just wanted to let you know that they felt like it would be important for the new girl to have a job in the church, so she's the one they chose."

"The new girl. Who sat with Mallory. Who didn't seem to sing lead or play an instrument," I said quietly. My toes sank into the soft carpet beneath me.

"Mmm-hmm," Walter said. "It'll be okay. They just don't realize how talented you are. I actually think they do, on some level, but just can't admit it. Or won't."

"Thanks. I'll see you tomorrow." I hung up the phone. Since Walter had left early, they must have called him to ask him to tell me. It was pretty cheap not to tell me themselves, even if Walter was a part of the praise team.

I didn't feel like praising. Maybe I shouldn't be on the praise team if I couldn't rustle up a smile and an "all will be well" feeling all the time. Grandma always says you can run to God or run away from Him; just be honest.

"Argh!" I didn't care if Janie or Justin heard me talking out loud to God. "Why do the populars always have to win? Is that very Christian? I can't understand it, Lord." I punched the pillow and let the tears stream down my face.

"Did you give me a gift to sing and write music to praise you, or is that just something I do? When I sing, I feel you. When I write, I feel you. But you won't let me share it anywhere. So what's the point?"

I shredded a piece of paper on my desk. It was to have been a new song. "What's the point of writing anymore? What's the point of taking piano anymore? I'm through with music. It's done nothing for me all these years. Let's face it. I stink. I'm a failure."

In the corner of my room, my ten notebooks were stacked—where I'd dumped them from my backpack when I got home. I scooped them up and headed for the burn barrel. Time to die.

I walked down the hallway, where Justin's sports trophies lined the shelves and where Janie had already tacked up one college acceptance letter. What did I have to show for all these years? The same old certificates that the piano teachers gave *everyone* who participated in the recitals? No. Enough was enough.

I huffed out to the backyard. When you live out of town a bit like we do, you can burn your paper trash. You just use a really big metal garbage can, a fifty-five-gallon drum, and throw it all in. When it gets full enough, a parent sets it on fire and *poof*. Cremation.

My mom tried to stop me, but I waved her off, careful not to look her in the eye so we didn't have to have a conversation. She stuck my piece of mail into my hands. I took it and stuffed it in my pocket to read later. Right now I was on a mission to burn every song I'd ever written since I was six years old.

The burn barrel was already lit. Bummer. That meant my dad was there.

"Paige!" Yep, he saw me. No turning back now. I carefully set the journals to the side of the porch and moved forward. I took a deep breath, tucked my hair behind my ears, and tried to look normal. Maybe we'd chat, he'd leave, and I could toss the whole stack of notebooks into the fire. If I brought them out now, we'd just have to talk about why I was burning them and how being a teenager was hard but it would pass. *Sigh*.

He didn't say much. It was so weird that even *I* thought I'd better start the conversation. Maybe then he'd go inside. "How is work—busy saving the world, or at least all the crops in Western Idaho and Eastern Washington?" Dad was the operating manager of Rainmaker, a company that made sprinkler systems.

"Yes," he said as he stirred the fire. Little bits of crackling flew out of the barrel like fireflies, dying as they hit the cold air. That's all he said. "Yes." The bitter smoke and ash rose into the sky like a prayer.

He sighed a bit more and stirred the fire again. It seemed like he'd forgotten I was there. He wasn't leaving the burn barrel any time soon. I decided to grab my notebooks and take them back into my room. I'd tiptoe out later when he was done.

Once in my room I opened the letter. "Dear Miss Winsome," it began.

> As you know, Christmas is a lonely time for many elderly people who have little or no family to share the joy. This year the shelter is planning to match an elderly resident of Lewiston with an abandoned or unwanted pet. For your contribution of two hundred dollars, a lonely pet and a

lonely person will have a Christmas they will always remember. The contribution will help pay for medical expenses and food for the first year—something these folks can't afford on their own. Please return this commitment card by October 15 so we can let our new homes have time to prepare. We will inform the waiting pet hopefuls as soon as we hear from you!

Well, *some* good was happening in the world. Even in my anger I felt a little corner of gladness. It was just like Mrs. Kellie and Kitty! I thought about how happy they were, how much easier it made her widowhood. And the little hamster and her Barbie home to come. It was a great idea. That's why I work with the shelter. They care.

Helping animals is one of the things I do best. I want to help people, too, because as much as I love pets, I care even more about people. I just don't talk about it all the time. That's why I write and sing—to share my love of music and love of God with other people. But *that* wasn't working out. "I wish I could do this, God. But I don't have two hundred dollars."

I tapped my keyboard and the screen came back on. I saw the email that I hadn't yet read. Oh yeah, the guitar. I guess I'd email back and say I didn't need one anymore. No need to learn guitar if I was done with music. Fifty dollars was all I had, and I'd need it for pet food and maybe to somehow try to scrape together one hundred fifty dollars more for the shelter's Christmas program. I opened the email.

> *Dear Paige,*
>
> *You don't know me, but I saw your post about wanting to buy a guitar. I have two now and really need to sell one, so you are an answer to prayer! I live in Clarkston, but maybe we can meet sometime—SOON—and I can get it to you. It's in great shape. You'll love it. Please email me ASAP.*
>
> > *Chordially,*
> > *Kate*

Chordially. So cool. Only a music person would think of that. Someone was counting on me to buy this guitar now, and she really needed to sell it for some reason. Did I want to email her back and tell her I couldn't do it? My hands trembled.

Before clicking the computer off, I saw a red note on the Worship Works site: "Singer-Songwriters! Try out!"

I read it further.

Calling all 13- to 16-year-old
Christian singer-songwriters
who live in the Snake River Valley.

Want to win $400 and sing at
half time at the annual Lewiston v. Clarkston
Thanksgiving Day football game?

That was the game Justin would play in! The game Britt and Mallory and everyone else I knew would be at. Dad would even come!

Since the winner will publicly perform,
preliminary singing auditions will be held
to narrow the field to five, and a
working draft of an original song must be
submitted. The final contestants will be
required to submit and perform an
original song. Apply today!

But I was quitting. Right? I closed my eyes and prayed. With four hundred dollars I could sponsor two pets with their new owners. Everyone would see that I could sing. I didn't want to be a star. I just wanted to be noticed as a part of the same universe as everyone else. For once I wanted to speak the language everyone else in my family speaks—success, importance, ability.

If I'm not seen, I can't be loved.

I believed this was brought right into my path on the very day I needed it. I felt faith flooding back into my heart again.

Dear Lord, I pleaded in my heart. *Just let me win this once. I will give the money away. I will not hog the spotlight. Just show me that you look upon the regular girls as well as the superstars. Let me know and I won't burn my journals. Show me by letting me win. Do you see me, Lord? Do you see me and love me? I want to win.*

I was overcome by the strongest sense of warmth and peace I had ever had. Ever! *It must be God. He must be saying that He's with me—that I should go ahead!*

I shut down my computer. Peace overwhelmed me like I had never felt before. I had faith! I took that faith and put it into action by signing the card to the shelter, committing to sponsor two animals—not one, but two—for elderly owners. I told them to go right ahead and share the good news. I ran down to the mailbox and mailed it before I could lose any bit of my newfound faith.

I stuck my journals back into my closet. "You're safe till Thanksgiving."

There was a lot at stake in this contest. The animals and their owners. My family, whom I needed to see me, to know me, to love me. Most of all, my faith in and relationship with God. If I lost, I could lose them all. But I wouldn't.

I had to win.

CHAPTER TWO
clarkston, washington

kate

I had to win.

If I didn't, then Mrs. Doyle would win. Mrs. Doyle, of course, is not between the ages of thirteen and sixteen, and as far as I know she can't play a note, write a tune, or even sing on key. But that wouldn't matter, because she'd *still* win, in a way, and I wasn't going to let that happen. Never.

When I came home from school on Wednesday,

Dad was mowing—probably for the last time this fall. He had to be to work at Rainmaker Sprinklers across the river in Lewiston at three o'clock, so he was rushing up and down stripping the lawn of summer's last green, even though the pumpkins and squash already squatted together in a neighborly way on our porch. Dad didn't like working the three-to-eleven assembly shift. None of us liked his working it. If he didn't, though, he wasn't available during the day to be a pastor. *Most pastors don't have to work two jobs,* I regularly reminded God. I felt like God was maybe nodding sympathetically, but it didn't change anything.

Lee and Nancy, the next-door twins, ran over and threw some leaves from the ground at me. I tossed some back and we had a leaf war.

Lee's hands were cold. I rubbed them between mine to warm them up. "Don't you have any mittens?"

He shook his head. "Maybe next paycheck."

My heart hurt. Why should kids have to wait to get mittens? Why should a five-year-old need to know about pay periods? The kids in my neighborhood learned to make do. Chilly hands. Leaves for toys. I touched Nancy's pink cheek.

"Better get inside before you freeze," I said. I gathered up the prettiest bouquet of leaves I could find. "Take these inside. I'll come over later with some waxed paper. We'll stick the leaves between two pieces and iron them to make stained-glass windows."

They smiled and nodded, and I gave Lee a high five. He and Nancy walked back toward their house, sandwiching the leaves between their chubby hands so they wouldn't lose any.

Dad turned the lawn mower off when he saw me. He tugged a navy blue bandanna from his back pocket, wiping his forehead. "How's my little sweetheart?" he asked before stuffing it back. I kissed his cheek and he smelled of hay—more likely, the dying grass that speckled his shirt.

"I'm almost fourteen," I reminded him. "Maybe we should find another nickname." He saw the curve of my lip, though, and winked. I'm his only child; it's hard for him to see me grow up. I cut him a break.

"How was school?"

"Good," I said. "Got all of my homework done so I won't have to rush before youth group tonight."

"Good girl," Dad said. "Mom is looking forward to singing with the choir tonight. She's had a hard day. Her hands hurt."

"I'll rub them," I promised. Before Dad could yank the cord and start the mower again, I said, "I wish you were coming with us."

"I will be there with you," Dad said, "in spirit. My body, however, will be at Rainmaker assembling sprinklers and hoping to keep my job and put food on the table. Food for the soul during the day, food for the table in the evening."

Always preaching. He was a funny old thing with what I considered a typical pastor's 'do: short hair on the sides, none in the middle. He said studying Greek had been so hard it had burned the hair right off the top of his head. I wished he wouldn't joke like that all the time. Wait. I take that back. I don't want him to do it when other people are around, but I don't want him to stop at home.

I walked toward the house, or what I like to affectionately call the "Cozy Cottage." It's what real estate agents say when they don't want to say the place is so small a family of mice might get on one another's nerves. The oaks around the house towered like gruff telephone poles, and ivy snaked around their trunks. I'd mostly raked the leaves the night before. I'd have to get out there and do some more later so Mom wouldn't try to do it. The trees' leafy heads of fire bowed together and planned against winter. They tried it every year. It never worked.

When people think of Washington State, they always think of Western Washington—woods and mountains, rain, the ocean. Well, our Washington is very different. We have farmland and big old trees and rivers and four full seasons. People who live together and know one another. Places where you can see as far in one direction as you can drive in a day. Lilac and rose bushes older than grandmothers.

"Hi." I tossed my backpack in the hallway and

flipped off my shoes. Barefoot was best. No shoes. No socks.

Mom hunched over the computer. Her brown hair was tucked behind her ears, and her little diamond chip earrings twinkled in her ear lobes. Dad and I bought her those earrings two years ago. She hardly ever wore anything else. Come to think of it, I don't think she had another pair.

"Hi. I'm busy doing bills. There are already a couple of phone messages for you on the machine."

I kissed her cheek, headed into the kitchen, and opened the refrigerator. After slapping together a sandwich out of Velveeta cheese and Wonder Bread with mayo on one side and pickle relish on the other, I sat down at the kitchen table and pressed Play on the message machine.

"Hi, Kate. Do you need a ride to church tonight? Because if you do, it would be no problem for us to pick you up. I haven't actually asked my mom yet, but she wouldn't mind. Just call me back if you need a ride, or anything else. Otherwise, see you there. Um, that's all. Bye." I swallowed a bit of sweet-and-sour relish and used my tongue to dislodge a Wonder Bread ball from behind my teeth.

Daniel. If *Star Trek* was ever missing a Klingon, it would be Daniel, because he was always clinging on. He meant well. He never came right out and said it, but he had this idea that since he was a missionary kid and I was a pastor's kid we should grow up and get married and have all kinds of ministry babies. I'm not even fourteen yet. The idea creeps me out.

Message number two: "Hi, Kate. I was wondering—could I sing lead tonight? I feel like maybe it's my turn? I could learn so much from you; you have so much to share." *Sigh*. Vickie didn't even really know me. In fact, she used to snub me in school till they started going to our church, and then when she found out I sang and was the pastor's kid, she was all over wanting to be my friend. Which would be great if she actually knew anything about the person she wanted to be friends with. She didn't know anything at all about me, the real me. We were different in every way. I had long black hair, she had curly red hair. I was tall, she was tiny. I was casual. She was always girly-girl. I scrounged. She always had enough.

I finished up my sandwich and screwed the lid back on the mayo. I should have wiped off the lid.

My mom sighed, closed the checkbook wearily, and stood up. "We'll leave a bit early tonight, okay? I'm going to drive Dad to work, and then I'll come back and change." She clutched two or three white envelopes in her hand.

"Planning to mail them at the post office on the way to drop off Dad?"

"Mmm-hmm. Waiting till the last minute means I have to take them into town so they'll make it in time."

She looked at me. "Money might be getting tighter soon."

"What do you mean?"

Mom shook her head. "Dad will talk with you himself when he's ready. I shouldn't have said anything."

No kidding. I hate when people do that.

After they pulled out of the driveway, autumn fog gracefully disguising the age of the car, I turned on the computer. Several weeks later I connected with the Internet. Just kidding. Dial-up does take a long time, though, compared with the high-speed access at school.

What's new at the Worship Works Web site? One of my friends from church had started it before she'd gone to college last year; the site was especially for Clarkston and Lewiston. I checked in from time to time even though someone else was running it now. I had only a minute or two—I should run through my songs before church and restring the new guitar. It had been nice of the Doyles to give it to me; it was better than my old one, much as I had loved it. It's just that it was kind of awkward when Mr. Doyle stood up in front of the church during prayer time and gave thanks to God for giving it to them so they could give it to someone in need. Then when I show up with the new guitar, well, you know, so much for anonymous donations and confidential prayer requests.

I checked the site's message board.

Wanted:
Guitar. Keyboardist and songwriter wants
to learn to play guitar. Looking for a good used
guitar for sale. Please email Paige.

Then she left an email address.

Hmm. Hadn't thought of selling my old friend, but maybe the money would be good. I glanced at it, leaning silently over in the corner. Nah. But it was kinda sad that it was silent so often now. Guitars weren't meant to be mute.

An email arrived from Kyle, and I quickly opened it.

Dear Kate,

I hope you're still planning to come for Christmas. We've already sent out notices to the families who need to take advantage of the Wee Care for Kids Christmas program. It's very cool that you found a way to get gifts for twenty kids. I mean, that's $400! Most of these kids have very little. You and I can relate, right? Little Kate can't wait for you to come. My dad will get in touch with your dad about the dates and times— but what should I tell the children's minister? We're still a go? Lemme know.

Later,

Kyle

P.S. I'm glad you're coming, too. Not just Little Kate.

Right on! Nothing, and no one, could stop me. I e-mailed back faster than a kid fleeing a bee.

I'm totally up for it. Count on me. Go ahead and tell the children's minister I will be there and she can start planning. Tell your sister, "little" Kate, that I am psyched to see her.

I wasn't very well going to write that I was psyched to see him, too. Even if I was. He did write *Dear* Kate, after all.

Thanks for putting this together. I appreciate it. And you.

That was as far as I would go. Awesome!

I'd check out the rest of the Worship Works site later, maybe look for some song-writing techniques. I was trying to learn to write my own music. It'd be fun to sing my own song on the reservation, teach the kids how to do it. I love kids and have always wished I had a brother or a sister, but my mom and dad couldn't have any more kids. I decided God had given me the heart for children so I could share my love with other kids like me, who needed affection and reassurance. Last year when we'd visited Kyle's family on the Nez Perce reservation, I was struck by how happy the kids were with the smallest of Christmas gifts. It shouldn't have to be that way—to get so little at Christmastime. Kyle understood—he was like me. His dad was a pastor, too, a Nez Perce pastor. They'd never had money, either, like us.

I'd told Kyle about the Wee Care Christmas program that our church partners with. It works with donors to provide gifts for kids fom low-income families. We'd prayed that there would be money for the Nez Perce church, too. It was going to cost like four hundred dollars to sponsor twenty kids. Wee Care matches the funds, and then the kids get both a fabulous present and a kids' Bible.

No one had been sure where our part of the money was going to come from, but then good old Mrs. Doyle heard about it and offered to donate. I'd swallowed my gum and said thank-you. At least I was going, and the kids would have a first-class present. Kyle and I were old enough to know that Christmas wasn't only about gifts, but little kids deserved both.

Oh no, I'd been answering email and daydreaming too long. Youth group! "What do I wear?" I called out to the empty house, running into my room, late as usual. The hopeless task of deciding rolled around as dependably as the numbers on the clock dial.

I really should start caring more about putting my clothes away straight. You know, pants in a pants drawer, shirts in a shirt drawer, etc. Sometimes I think being careless is a way to say I don't care that my clothes are old when I really do care. You know? I grabbed a pair of khaki cargo pants that had seen better days, wishing I had a pink-striped belt to go with them. My pink rugby shirt was worn out at the elbows, and the collar was just a little yellowed. No one would notice. Or maybe they would. But what could I do? At least my GummyWears choker was fun. It looked like a piece of already-chewed gum on hemp strings. It always caught people's attention.

"I'm ready when you are." My mom had returned and was ironing her shirt. Do you know anyone else's mom who still irons her shirts? It's cool. Most people take theirs to the cleaners, but my mom does a great job. It helps the clothes last longer, she says.

We drove the few miles to church. It's not a big church, really. We like to call it the church that love built. Cheesy, I agree. I like going to a small church. I know everyone and they know me. There are enough of us, I think. It's kind of like family in that we love and fight and know everyone else's business. The only way it wasn't like family is that I didn't have a sister there. I had people around me, you know, that I could laugh with and stuff. But nobody deep. I longed for that.

Everyone at church ate dinner together near the small kitchen and then split up to go our separate ways.

"You guys ready?" I'd brought my guitar into the center of the teen room. Okay, so it used to be a large storage area and a leftover Sunday school classroom combined. We decorated it however we wanted, though, in tie-dye and posters and with a donated foosball table. We had great speakers, so the sound was good. It was big enough to hold all the new people who had been coming.

"Cute shirt," Vickie said after I'd finished leading the opening music. "I love it. Do you want to sit with us?"

"Yeah," I said. She dragged me over to where they'd made a circle with the chairs. Several other girls made space for me, which I appreciated, and cooed over my hair, which I didn't. 'Cause we're a smaller church, our high school and junior high meet together. Daniel's older brother leads the discussion. He's not a Klingon. Maybe when he moves out of the house Daniel will get a chance to shine. Vickie certainly wanted hers.

I love worship, and I worship best by singing, although other people connect better in other ways. Sometimes, and I feel guilty about this, I wish we could just sing and praise and go on and on the whole time like that. Then I think, yeah, well, if I wasn't learning anything about God, I'd just be doing it for the experience and not connecting. Then it'd be all about me.

"We're going to talk about Philippians because that's what Pastor is preaching on," Daniel's brother said.

Daniel smiled at me and kept brushing his too-long bangs out of his face. Vickie picked at her hangnails. Jessie Smith was okay. I usually sit by her. She doesn't sing, but she's nice and fun.

"Hey, you want to lead the closing song?" I said to Vickie toward the end.

She smiled. I felt good inside, and I guess part of me wasn't afraid to be nice to her because I knew she wasn't as good at singing lead as I am. Even if she never had to worry about money.

Afterward, as I was heading down to the sanctuary to get my mom, I heard, "Hellooo! Kate." I looked for a potential escape route and found none. I was trapped.

"Hi, Mrs. Doyle. How are you?"

"Fine, fine. Here." She thrust a big green garbage bag at me.

"Oh, I think Norm will take out the trash," I said.

"No, dear, these are clothes. I know that your mom can use some; I can see that. I gathered some old things from my closet and a few dear friends. Friends that don't attend here, of course. Not that your mother would mind anyway. She's so sweet. And, of course, she's certainly aware that beggars can't be choosers."

I dropped the bag like my hand was on fire. Mrs. Doyle looked at me but said nothing. *Yeah, right,* I thought.

"Harvey and the kids and I all did without major souvenirs on our summer vacation this year to save money so you can buy gifts for those unfortunates on the reservation this Christmas." She looked at me and smiled. Stomach juice rose in my throat. Someone sent the Christmas fruitcake early. Her.

Unfortunates? I don't think so. She had no idea. You know, sometimes being impulsive is bad. Answering email to cute guys right away without thinking can come back to haunt you. Speaking up in class before figuring out the answer looks dumb and can sting later. I wished I had thought before I answered Mrs. Doyle. But now the fire feeling had traveled from my hand to my heart to my mouth. Dissing me was one thing. Dissing my mother and my friends was another. My honor was at stake.

"My mother has lots of clothes, and I don't need the money for the reservation anymore. But thank you anyway."

She looked at me with her mouth open and then closed it again. Her lips were still lined but her lipstick had worn off, so it looked really odd.

"Well, that's nice, dear," she stammered. "Are you still going?"

"Yes," I said, hoping mightily that it was true. "Have a nice night."

Now the burning feeling was in my stomach. What had I just done? First I promised Kyle and the kids, and now I just cut off the funds to get the gifts.

Mom was quiet on the way home. A light rain spattered against the leaves slipping to the ground. Mom's candy scented the air with peppermint. Finally I spoke.

"Dad said your hands hurt today."

"Yes, but I'll be okay." My mom had early onset arthritis. Her once beautiful hands were bent and twisted like a wrung-out dishrag.

"You don't have to work tomorrow, do you?" I asked. Sometimes my mom worked in a nursery caring for plants. The owner was a friend and was flexible around my mom's arthritis flare-ups.

"Nope," Mom said. "Let's watch a movie together after you get your pj's on and before I have to go pick up Dad."

"Okay. I'll rub your hands." We watched a library or garage-sale movie together almost every night. She always let me pick the title. I knew what we'd be watching that night: *How the Grinch Stole Christmas!*

When we got home, I logged on to my email right away and started a new message. I knew where fifty of the four hundred dollars I needed was going to come from.

Dear Paige,

You don't know me, but I saw your post about wanting to buy a guitar. I have two now and really need to sell one, so you are an answer to prayer! I live in Clarkston, but maybe we can meet sometime—SOON—and I can get it to you. It's in great shape. You'll love it. Please email me ASAP.

Chordially,
Kate

Just before clicking off, I saw a red note on the site: "Singer-Songwriters! Try out!"

> Calling all 13- to 16-year-old
> Christian singer-songwriters
> who live in the Snake River Valley.
> Want to win $400 and sing at
> the annual Lewiston v. Clarkston
> Thanksgiving Day football game?

Four hundred plus fifty equals ... four hundred fifty dollars! I'd get the money to go to the reservation with the gifts for the kids! Playing before the crowd at the game would be good experience—and maybe I could even open in a prayer or something to bring God into it. I knew from talking with Kyle's friends in Seattle that this would never fly in a big city, but small towns still felt okay with God.

> Since the winner will publicly perform,
> preliminary singing auditions will be held
> to narrow the field to five, and a
> working draft of an original song must be
> submitted. The final contestants will be
> required to submit and perform an
> original song. Apply today!

After clicking on the application page, I prayed before

typing in my information. "Lord, you know how much I need that money," I whispered. "The kids on the reservation are counting on me to help them celebrate Christmas. I can love them, the kids you gave to me instead of brothers and sisters. I can honor you this way."

The rest I prayed in my head. It just felt more private.

I'm sorry that I snapped at Mrs. Doyle, I really am. I was stupid. But you know, I can only handle so much. At some point my back is just cracked. Look at my dad, Lord. He's working hard. My mom's hands are almost useless. They praise you. I love you. Can we please have some dignity for once, to serve others without having to take charity ourselves? Show me, Lord, that you honor those who have little as well as those who have a lot. I want to win.

After I was done praying, I was overcome by the strongest sense of warmth and peace I had ever had. Ever. It must be God. He must have been saying that He was with me—that I should go ahead! I believed this was brought right into my path on the very day I needed it. I felt faith flooding back into my heart again.

There was a lot at stake in this contest. Christmas for the kids on the reservation—like Katie. Kyle! My family, who needed honor and dignity in the midst of all that they gave to others. A time to shine. A chance to see that God cares for the small and lowly and not just the high and mighty. Because, most of all, my faith in and relationship with God were at stake. If I lost, I could lose them all. The world was not populated by musical dabblers like Vickie, though. There were people with real talent who were sure to enter the contest.

Whom would I compete against?

CHAPTER THREE
lewiston, idaho

paige

Whom would I compete against?

What does God do when lots of Christians try to win the same thing? He can't play favorites. That's what this whole thing was about for me, knowing in my heart that God doesn't favor populars and other Rapunzel types. And about providing pets for lonely people and people for lonely animals, of course, because they're unpopular, too. I needed to know He cared, that He was there. Birds of the air, fishes in the sea, and people like me. I was going to make it happen.

So you see why, a little more than a week later, on a blustery Saturday night, I just wanted everyone out of the house. I couldn't compose with all the craziness going on at home. I needed quiet to write.

"Are you staying home *again* tonight?" Janie strode into my room. Speaking of Rapunzel types. Brown-haired ones, anyway.

"Yes, I'm practicing," I said. Normally her question would have really bugged me, but not tonight. I had one goal in mind. I'd start just as soon as they all left.

"What is *this* doing in here?" Janie blew by me like the north wind of November to grab her new beige sweater off my bed.

"I hoped I could borrow it for the tryouts. To look and feel really good. I was trying it on to see if it fit." That sweater cost eighty dollars or something. It felt so good against my skin, like cuddling a bunny. Of course, I don't wear any real fur of any kind, bunny or otherwise.

"I don't *think* so." She held it tightly. "What's wrong with your new red one? It's cute."

"Nothing. I'm saving that for the last tryouts, when they get down to the final five competitors. Since it's my favorite."

"Well, I'm glad you're feeling confident that you'll make it to the final tryouts. But I'm not sharing this." She turned to go. "You should have asked."

"'All the believers were of one heart and mind, and they felt that what they owned was not their own; they shared everything they had,'" I yelled after her, but she'd slammed the door. "Acts 4:32!" I knew that was the verse she'd learned in high school hour last Sunday because they learned the same verses that we did. We were both memorizing, too, because it got us credit toward a discount on the upcoming ski trip, even though Mom and Dad would have paid for it in full if we'd needed them to.

Mr. Hair Gel walked down the hall, whistling.

"You smell good," I said and meant it. He must have put on cologne or something. I didn't expect him to actually stop and acknowledge my presence.

"Heard about the contest. Cool," he said. He picked up one of the dog's squish balls and tossed it at me. "Told my friends that my sister might sing at half time, and they thought it was cool, too."

I wanted to beam, but that would give him too much satisfaction. Instead, I chucked the squish ball back at him. He grinned so I knew he understood. I kind of wished he hadn't told his friends, though. What if I didn't even make the first tryouts? That had happened once before. I tried out for girls' lacrosse and didn't make it, and then we had to tell everyone.

Then I tried softball. Struck out. People just said, "Oh, *so* sorry," and "*Bad* news," like non-athleticism was a disease or handicap of some sort.

Speaking of natural talent, Janie and Justin were heading out for the night. Mom was finishing up her makeup, and Dad sat on the couch tapping his shoes against the floor. He'd shined his shoes and was wearing a new tie.

"Still ticking?" I asked. He'd looked at his watch ten times.

"Yeah."

"I heard things aren't so great at work. Mom told me."

"No, the company isn't doing well. We're meeting tonight with my boss and some people who might invest money into the company to keep it going."

"What if they don't invest money?" All of a sudden it felt like I'd yanked my ponytails too tight. My head hurt and my heart raced. My dad had always worked for Rainmaker. There weren't many companies in Lewiston that large. What would Dad do? What would *we* do?

"If the company we meet with tonight doesn't invest money, then the company will be shut down. All of our people will lose their jobs."

"What about us?"

"Management would, too," Dad admitted.

That meant *us*! I knew Dad's heart was concerned

about the hundreds of people who worked assembling and building. Rainmaker was one of the largest employers in the Snake River Valley; we have so many farms around and a port to ship stuff out of. Maybe if he thought about them, he wouldn't have time to worry about us.

"We're having a company meeting next Saturday at the Grange Hall," he went on, "to discuss the situation with all of the employees on both shifts. I hope I have something good to share. We're going to run out of cash."

"Soon?"

Dad nodded. "Soon."

"Good luck tonight," I said and scooted closer toward him on the couch. He didn't even shoo Brie off the couch and instead let her sit next to him. Either he was distracted, forgot he didn't like animals too much, or felt, like me, that puppy love was okay in times of looming disaster. Silently I prayed for my dad.

Later, the taillights of the car winked down the driveway into the fog, and Brie and I ran downstairs. "It's time, girl!"

Brie barked and settled into her cushion. I gave her a chicken chewy and she began to gnaw.

The lights were dim, and the room was neither too cool nor too warm. Even though we'd remodeled it into a family room, it still smelled a little like a basement. You know, slightly like fresh dirt or something.

I closed my eyes and prayed and asked the Lord to come near to me. I turned on some music and listened and let it carry me away to another place, to a place where it would be easier to start my own music. Then I sat down at the piano and laid a hand on it like I once held hands with my dad when I was little—barely touching fingertip to keyboard but still connected. I began to play and compose words in my head.

> I hear your music everywhere,
> The rhythmic strokes as I brush my hair,
> My pounding heart beating out despair.
> I hear you.
> I hear you.
> Like the Pied Piper,
> I can follow you
> Anywhere.

The music came from my fingertips. It was mysterious. God is the Creator of everything, and He was asking me if I'd like to join Him in creating music. He made it happen over and over again. His hands on mine, just like my very first piano teacher. She'd set my hands on the keyboard and then put her hands over them to show me how to gently touch the keys—not too hard, not too soft, and then adjust.

God's hands were over mine now in a way I'd never felt before. I knew that the words of every opening line were going to be the refrain, and that it would change. I'd never written a song like that before. It was totally, awesomely new. At least to me. I knew He was giving this song to me.

After writing down what I had so far, I did what all great composers do. I watched movies for a couple of hours and ate leftovers! Moo shoo tofu rolled up in thin pancakes dunked in sticky plum sauce—or "yum" sauce, as Janie and I liked to call it.

Speaking of Janie . . .

I might just try on that beige sweater again or look in her room for something else. She probably wouldn't be home for a while yet. Then I'd email Maddie, my very best friend from sixth grade, who had moved to Hawaii two years ago. I missed her, but I'd kind of forgotten what she looked and sounded like. I needed someone here. Close by. Maybe I should check and see if that Kate girl wanted to get together soon and trade cash for the guitar. Hey! Imagine what my new song would sound like on the guitar.

I looked at the clock. I might have time before Janie had to be home. She wasn't allowed to stay out as late on Saturday night as on Friday night, since we had to be at church on Sunday.

I opened her bedroom door, then called to the dog, and we both flopped on Janie's bed. I loved that bed. It was a wrought-iron daybed with an attached trundle bed that scooted underneath like a skittish cat whenever you didn't need it. I let the dog lie on the bed. Janie'd die if she knew. I wanted a wrought-iron daybed. Not this one. My own.

The beige sweater was good, but so was the baby blue one. I wasn't sure if baby blue was my best color, though. Dark hair and dark eyes look better with beiges, reds, and oranges, at least according to that beauty book I'd checked out of the library. Janie had no orange sweater that I knew of. It'd have to be beige. It was awesome. I wondered if Mom was going to buy an eighty-dollar sweater for me when I was a senior or if I'd be counting my blessings to get Janie's old ones four years later.

Sigh. I was kidding myself. I'd wear something old to the first tryout, and if I made the cut, I'd wear the red one to the final tryout to celebrate.

I logged on. Being on the computer made it less lonely to be home alone. It could get kinda scary later at night. I ran and closed the blinds as the nearly naked tree limbs tapped bony fingers against the windowpane. I wished Mom and Dad would get home from their business dinner.

Hey! There was a message from Maddie and one from Kate.

I opened Kate's first.

> *If it's at all possible, could I bring the guitar over to your house this week? We go to Lewiston almost every day to drop my dad off at work. Also, he has a company meeting next Saturday at the Grange Hall, and I could do it then if weekdays don't work for you. Whichever works best for you would be great for me. Let me know either way.*
>
> > *Chordially,*
> > *Kate*

Usually I sat on my email for a day or two before answering, but not tonight. I wrote back.

> *Does your dad work for Rainmaker Sprinklers? My dad does, and he's got a meeting at Grange Hall next Saturday. If that's the meeting you're talking about, maybe we could meet there. Cool. Write back soon.*
> *Paige*

I knew by the way my dad dragged around the house all week that the meeting with the potential investors hadn't been good. Plus, my mom made stuffed mushrooms one night and asparagus wrapped in ham and cream cheese another. She never let him eat high-cholesterol foods unless there was something bad going on. Then she gave in to comfort. As for me, I was just glad she was cooking and not ordering takeout. On Saturday I thought I'd see if she'd slip any information about the company my way if I brought up the topic.

"I'm coming to the meeting tonight, right?" I asked, sitting on the breakfast barstool, doodling on my homework. I drew a picture of a poodle dressed in a scarf and sunglasses, flagging down help while her new, rattling car sat by the side of the road. Then I doodled a picture of a sheep dog who worked too hard trying to care for all his sheep and never made it back to the house and his family.

"Oh yes, I'd completely forgotten." My mom wiped her hands on a dish towel. "You're meeting that girl to buy her guitar?" Suddenly it all seemed like too much. She always "completely forgot" what was going on in my life!

"Mom," I asked. "Do you remember when we were all really little and you had to split a can of fruit cocktail between all of us?"

She stopped with the dishes and looked at me as

if she might need to take my temperature. "Yes."

"Well, sometimes I feel like when you're dividing up your time, Janie and Justin get all the cherries and grapes, and I get the mushy pears."

"Oh," she said. She didn't say anything else, but I knew she was thinking. Then I knew she was uncomfortable because she switched topics. "Do you think it'll be okay to meet that girl? I mean, we don't know anything about her."

"I don't think she's going to hack me into pieces in the parking lot," I said. "We'd know where to find her dad."

Mom laughed, and I laughed with her. "I'll give you some money and you can run next door to Two Trees Chinese and eat dinner while the meeting is going on. It might get, um, loud, and not a good place for two girls to be."

Loud. I hadn't thought there would be fights or anything. Things must be worse off at the company than Dad had told us. In fact, I don't ever remember their holding a meeting like this before.

I went back upstairs and unfolded five ten-dollar bills that I'd been saving for pet food, shots, and stuff. But if I won—and I might even be able to pick some chords on the guitar for the contest—I could place two pets for life. I could always pick up some donated food at the shelter. And I'd made a commitment to buy the guitar whether or not I used it in the contest.

Time to pick an outfit: army green cargo pants, not too baggy, not too tight; feminine white T-shirt with squiggly writing on it; brown clogs. My hair went back in ponytails, low, of course. Then a little shine powder and some lip gloss—not too shiny or too pink, didn't want to look like Barbie. I was ready to go. We got into the car and drove off. I wondered what Kate would be like. I knew she liked music. She was already high on my list.

The main thing about Lewiston is that it's on the east bank of the Snake River. The Snake River splits Washington and Idaho. I live in Idaho, of course. Kate lives in Clarkston, Washington, right across the river. Lewis and Clark. Our town has tall maples, brick-lined streets, and lots of new houses; Clarkston has trees, too, of course, but not as many. Their houses are older.

Both towns have hills that are scalped in green and brown and the color of dried corn. It's cold in the winter and hot in the summer and I love it. I hoped I never had to leave. Afternoon fog crept in while we drove, the cool of the river clashing with the heat the land had soaked up like sauna stones during the day.

"Is fifteen dollars enough?" Mom asked.

I gaped. Yes! Tea was free, of course. I didn't want

to say anything because she looked like she was try-ing to be generous. If my dad lost his job, that would be the end of dinners out, so I might as well take it. "Thanks, Mom."

"Maybe we can go shopping or walking or some-thing next week," Mom said. Then she bit her lip. "Of course, there's the booster meeting for Justin's foot-ball team, and Janie has to take in her financial aid papers. I don't know what Dad's got planned, with all the trouble that's going on. I can't keep track. Ladies Bible Study has a planning meeting. But," she said, "we'll squeeze some time in somehow."

Yep.

We pulled into the parking lot of the Grange Hall. What would she look like? How would I know it was her?

Duh. She'd be carrying the guitar case.

I saw her standing right outside the hall. "Hi," I said. "I'm Paige. Are you Kate?"

She nodded. "Yes! I forgot to tell you what I looked like, but then I thought of course you'd rec-ognize the guitar. It's nothing fancy, and I need the case back."

"Oh, that's okay," I said. "Cases cost a lot." She was pretty and tall, and her clothes were stylish but didn't call out, "Look at me!" Her hair was pulled back into a thick black ponytail, and she had a sprinkling of light freckles across her face like cinnamon on sugar.

"Would you like me to put that into the car before the meeting starts?" Mom said.

"Just give me the keys," I said. "I'll do it." I got really brave. I mean, I never invited anyone, except Maddie, to do anything. What if she said no?

"I'm going next door to have Chinese food for dinner. At Two Trees." I motioned toward it. "Would you like to come?"

Kate looked at her mom, and a weird funky looked passed between them. Oh great. This was exactly why I don't invite people. She thought I was glomming on trying to be her friend after five minutes. Or maybe she knew that my dad was the operating manager and her dad didn't like him because of all this company stuff.

Her mom shrugged her shoulders.

"Okay," Kate said. "I'm not hungry, but I could come and have tea."

The moms went inside, I locked up the guitar, and we walked to Two Trees.

"So you won't miss this guitar?" I asked as we sat down.

I ordered vegetarian stir-fry with noodles. No meat for me. Ever. Kate ordered tea.

"Yeah, but I'm saving money to go to the Nez Perce reservation and help organize Christmas gifts for the kids this Christmas. I have to save three hundred fifty dollars more, though."

Kate looked really well put together, but now that I looked closely, I noticed her clothes looked kind of old. I had noticed the car they drove up in, too. It was way older than Janie's. Suddenly I realized why she might not be hungry. No spending money!

"Do you want some of my meal?" I asked. "I will feel like a total pig eating by myself while you're sitting here. Really."

"Oh, that's fine. Thanks anyway."

Maybe she was one of those constant dieters.

When it came, though, the waitress must have assumed we were splitting, as she brought an extra plate. I held it out to Kate with a question in my eyes. She looked at my plate and said, "Well, maybe just a little. If you don't mind sharing."

"Not at all," I said. "Here." I scooped some onto the extra plate. "I hope you don't mind if it's vegetarian."

"I like all kinds of food," Kate said, laughing. "Maybe too much."

Some kids came in and called out, "Hey, Katie!" She laughed with them, a group of guys and girls, and talked for a little while. They waved to her and left with some takeout. We went back to eating, but soon some more people came in and greeted her. She didn't even live in Lewiston and she knew more people than I did. I wondered if she was a popular.

"So your dad works at Rainmaker?" I asked.

"Yes, but mainly he's a pastor. He works there, too, because our church is small."

Oh. A popular pastor's daughter. I narrowed my eyes. She didn't *seem* like the Mallory type.

"Well, I knew you were a Christian because you saw my notice on the Worship Works site."

"My friend started it," Kate said. "I got to help her. She's the one who put the ad up at Rainmaker. Is that where you saw it?" Her eyes sparkled as she talked, and now that we had gotten going, she talked more than I did.

I nodded.

"She's at college now, but I check in every once in a while. I love worship, especially singing."

"Me too!" I said. "Hardly any of my friends do, though. Not like I do."

"Mine either," Kate said, and we smiled together. "I know what you mean." She named several songs she liked and I started humming. She sang low under her breath and I harmonized.

"Oh," I said. I looked up and half the restaurant was staring. We both burst out laughing.

"Who cares?" she said. "Not me."

"Me neither," I said. Her confidence was contagious.

We talked about movies we both loved, and she

told me that she had a crush on one of the Christian boys at the reservation, and I told her about Walter. "Even though he likes me, I don't like him," I said. "Too weak." I doodled a man trying to do a flexed arm hang. "Not in his body, I mean, just that he never stands up for anything. I don't really care if I have a crush on anyone, but if I do, it's not going to be a wimp. It'll be someone who's not afraid to speak up."

"I have a feeling that's exactly who you'll find," Kate said. She smiled and I smiled back.

It seemed like whatever we talked about we both liked. Well, there were a few differences. She loved kids and wished she had a brother or sister. I loved animals and wished my brother and sister were gone. Hey! Being a little different makes things even more interesting.

Two girls wearing matching soccer sweat shirts walked in and sat down together.

"One thing about being into music is that I sometimes feel left out." I nodded toward their matching hoodies. "You know?"

Kate wrinkled her brow. "I never feel left out of anything."

My heart sank, and it must have shown on my face, because she said, "But I know what you mean. We musicians should have something, too."

"Not a sweat shirt," I said.

Kate shook her head and looked around. "It

should have something to do with music." She reached over and grabbed the extra set of chopsticks. "Like these!"

Chopsticks? I wondered. "Oh—like the song 'Chopsticks.'" I got it.

"I knew you'd get it!" she said.

I laughed and took them from her outstretched hand. "Even though people don't understand it, music is not a solitary sport, is it?"

"Nope," she agreed. "You just have to find the right team."

I broke the two chopsticks apart and gave one to her and kept one for myself. She took it and slid it into her long black ponytail. I undid my hair from the two ponytails and made them into one and followed suit.

"Are we a team?"

We shook hands. "We are," I agreed.

We finished up and cracked open our fortune cookies.

"'Excitement lies ahead,'" I read. "Excitement? Not in my life."

"Would you like to meet at the mall sometime, go shopping? It's not really exciting, I know, but it might be fun," Kate offered. "And we could stop by the music store."

How cool. "I'd love to."

Kate opened her cookie and then slipped the fortune into her pocket. She looked very sad.

"Come on," I said. "I read mine to you!"

She shrugged and then read it. "'Your helpfulness will be well rewarded.'"

"I can see that about you already," I said. She hardly knew me and was already making my fortune come true—and look at those kids on the reservation. Why was she sad?

After I'd paid my bill, we walked outside. I wanted to share my good news with her since she did seem like an honest, true friend already.

Kate slowed down. I kept talking.

"It's kind of like I was saying, music people get left out a lot. Especially in my family. But there's this contest, and if I win, it will allow everyone at the Thanksgiving game to see how important music is to me. And that it counts. Plus, I have good plans for the money. I haven't told you about my pets yet."

Kate looked at me. "I'm entering that contest, too."

Oh.

I suppose it was only natural. I mean, the only reason we even knew about each other was because we'd both looked at the same Web site. We were both Christians. We both liked music.

"Well, I'm glad," I said. I was. Kind of. "It won't change anything for us, will it?"

I felt sick to my stomach. Finally a great friend, a

musical friend, a Christian friend who wanted to help me as much as I wanted to help her. I felt like we were close buddies even though we'd just met, and the popular thing didn't seem to matter at all.

"No," Kate agreed. We walked out to the parking lot together, having fun, but laughing a little less easily. I saw her look at me out of the corner of her eye once, but only because I was looking at her out of the corner of mine.

In a perfect world competition wouldn't change friendships.

CHAPTER FOUR
clarkston, washington

kate

In a perfect world competition wouldn't change friendships. Now it was complicating almost every friendship I had. Paige. Vickie.

I was standing in the hall getting some books out of my locker the next Tuesday afternoon when I heard some kids talking about my church. I left my locker door open so they couldn't see me and slowly got my books out. I couldn't help overhearing. I mean, they were right next to me.

"I've heard of that church," one girl said. "I think Vickie is the singer for the youth group there. Maybe we should visit one Wednesday night. She's really cool, so it must be a really cool church."

So. Vickie was *the* singer. No mention of the rest of us. I walked home slowly, down the lane to the cottage, careful not to squash slugs in the gutter. They had a lowly life, too. Underdogs of the gardening world. Some boys I knew sprinkled salt on them just to watch them die. I didn't want to take anything away from them. It was a hard life, being a slug.

"Hi!" my mom said as I walked in. She must be feeling better. There were homemade peanut butter cookies on the counter—my favorite. It was hard for her to mash the fork prints on top of them when her hands hurt. I loved them, though, because every cookie had a cross on it. They've always been my favorite. Today, though, I couldn't look at the cross too long. I bit in and let the grainy feel of the cookie take over my senses so I could ignore God pressing on my heart.

After I washed the cookie down with some milk, I told my mom, "We're doing some new songs at youth group tomorrow night. I'd like to practice them."

"Okay, honey. Oh! There's a phone message for you," Mom replied. "And mail." She flapped an envelope at me. The contest form!

First the phone call. I pressed Play.

"Hi, Kate, this is Carrie at church. I was wondering if you'd be able to sit with the kids tomorrow night while the choir practices. We're working hard on the Christmas program, and our regular baby-sitter can't come tomorrow night. If we can't offer childcare, some of our members won't be able to attend. Please let me know. Don't worry if you can't. I'll be able to look for someone else. I just know how much you like kids. Bye!"

Well, tomorrow night was youth group. And we were working on new songs, too. Maybe Carrie didn't know that. An image of the kids at the locker next to mine passed by my eyes. Maybe they would be there tomorrow night. I really should lead music.

I called Carrie back and left a message. "I'm sorry, Carrie," I said. "I have to lead music in youth group. Otherwise I would. Keep me in mind for other times, okay?" I hung up before she could pick up the phone just in case she was there.

I had one more call to make before I headed upstairs to practice my songs. "Hi, Paige, this is Kate. I wondered if you still wanted to meet this week. Let me know." I left my number and hung up. Maybe she was just being nice at dinner and didn't really want to get together. It hadn't seemed like that, though.

I walked into my room and fingered the rough wooden chopstick on my desk. Paige was the first girl my own age I'd ever met that truly loved music. Could our new friendship survive this? It was just that we'd really connected. Usually new friends take a long time to feel comfortable with each other, but not this time. I had other friends, and she did, too, but it was so great to have a musical friend for once. She was willing to share—like her dinner. She didn't make me feel bad about buying my guitar. She didn't rub it in that her dad was the manager of the company. She liked to laugh. She was the kind of person who had everything and still knew how to share. I admired that. I wanted to make it work, for both of us. I just didn't know how. I was afraid it wouldn't be possible no matter what we tried.

Sliding my finger under the envelope seal, I opened the letter. All of a sudden I pulled back. You never knew who had licked it shut, and now I had just rubbed the dry spit on my fingers. Gross! I shook the page open and read it.

> *Dear Miss Kennedy,*
> *We're glad that you'll be able to try out for the Turkey Bowl competition. Please arrive at the Clarkston high school at 4:00 next Monday afternoon. Be prepared to sing "The Star-Spangled Banner" and have a copy of a song you've written. The final five contestants will face off the first week of November. Best wishes.*
> *Worship Works Staff*

Right on! I was going to win. I knew it. I felt that warm,

tingly feeling all over again, and I sang better practicing at home that night than I ever had before. Not only would I have enough money to get the kids' presents, but with the money I'd gotten from selling my guitar, I'd have money to buy my mom and dad something for Christmas, too. Maybe even Lee and Nancy! I'd have to bring them some peanut butter cookies. They loved them, too. Like me.

Even poor people can have dreams come true. Every kid at Kyle's church would celebrate Jesus' birthday with a gift this year, and when we talked about the Lord being a special present to the world, they would all truly understand what it meant.

That night Mom and I watched *Willy Wonka and the Chocolate Factory* and licked the chocolate from our fingers while I neatly folded the gold wrapper from the Wonka bar that Mom had picked up from the drugstore.

Wednesday night we got to church a bit late. Mom had had some phone calls to make before we blew out of the house into the dusky evening.

At the church, I grabbed my guitar and headed down the hall while stuffing a cookie into my mouth. I could hear someone tinkering on the electric keyboard. As I walked by the nursery, I saw Vickie sitting on the floor with some of the kids, playing patty-cake and quietly singing. I had misjudged Vickie. Why? Because she seemed to have everything, and I had only *one* thing and didn't want it taken away.

The cookies turned to crumbs in my mouth, dry, bitter, tasteless. If I hadn't been in public, I would have spat them out. Vickie didn't see me. She'd said yes to Carrie. I felt like a slug. With salt.

The kids who had been talking at the lockers the day before weren't there, either. My beautiful, strong voice of the night before seemed a little off-key tonight. Daniel and Jessie chatted over in the corner, and I felt left out. I walked up to them. "Can I sit over here?"

"Sure!" Jessie said.

Mom and I cleaned up the church after everyone else had left. Finally Mom locked up and we drove home. She chatted on about the Christmas cantata and asked how my night had gone.

"Good." The contest was on my mind. Vickie was on my mind. Seeing Paige soon was on my mind. Things somehow seemed more complicated today than they had yesterday.

Friday arrived quickly. How would things be between Paige and me? After I'd called her on Tuesday, we'd emailed back and forth every day. We chatted about nothing—and everything! We'd made a plan to walk the park trail on her side of the river, the Lewiston side, after school today before the weather turned icky, and then maybe we'd do the mall once it got too cold to be outside. Mom dropped us off there after she'd taken Dad to work. We'd picked Paige up at the same time; she had been waiting in her dad's office. My mom was going to do some shopping and then pick us both up at the park again and take Paige back to her dad's office. Her dad was high up there. My dad didn't have an office.

"Did you get your letter?" Paige drew hers out of her pocket. The wind blew mist off the river like my mom blew steam off a spaghetti pot, but my hair stayed put. I'd twisted my hair back into a tight ponytail and slipped the chopstick through. I was totally psyched to see that, without our even planning it, Paige had done the same thing.

"Yes. I'm surprised that they asked us to sing 'The Star-Spangled Banner.' Why, do you think?" I asked.

"Maybe they'll have us sing it at the opening?" Paige said.

I snapped my fingers. "You're probably right. What

about the original song you have to submit?" I pulled my sweat jacket more closely to me and withdrew my hands into my sleeves. We walked by while the river, calm on top, turbulent underneath, churned by, carrying its secrets downstream.

"I have a song I wrote a little while ago," Paige said. "I have notebooks and notebooks of them. . . ." Her voice trailed off. "Anyway, I'm writing a new one now called 'Follow Me.' I think it'll be my best one. I'm doing it on the computer with my music writing program."

"Oh." I didn't have a music writing program or notebooks full of songs. "I have a good one I wrote to God last Easter," I said. "I've never sung it to anyone but Him."

Paige looked at me and twisted her chopstick to tighten her dark brown hairdo in the wind, then smiled. I don't think she knew she was pretty; she acted like a girl who didn't think too much of herself. But she was pretty, especially when she smiled and her dimples flashed. More important, she was kind. She might not have meant anything by twisting the chopstick, but to me it said, "Hey, we're a team."

"Can I sing it to you?" I asked, hoping I didn't sound stupid. I didn't usually go around offering to sing to my friends, after all.

"I was hoping you'd say that," she said. "I didn't want to ask in case it was too private between you and God."

She understood. She writes to God, too.

No one else walked the trail on that chilly fall day; we

had the river to one side and trees to the other. I sang loud. I forgot Paige was there till I was done.

She stared at me quietly. Oh man. I hoped I hadn't embarrassed her.

"You have the most powerful, on-key voice I have ever heard," she said. She had a sweet smile as she said it, but I saw something else in her eyes. Fear? Sorrow? I don't know. I didn't know her well enough to read those kinds of things yet.

So instead we talked about dogs—hers—and boys. "I've never had one," I said. "I'm kind of afraid of them."

Paige laughed. "Dogs or boys?" she asked. We both cracked up. "My dog weighs seven pounds. She's a Havanese. You wouldn't be afraid of her. Just bring her some Kentucky Fried Chicken. She's addicted. She'll be your buddy for life."

Was she inviting me over to her house?

I told her more about Kyle. "We met years ago because our dads went to Bible school together. They don't have much. I admire them. They live the way the Bible says Christians should live—everyone helping everyone else."

Paige gave me a slanted look. "Great, glad they're so handy. Get to the part about Kyle."

I grinned. She knew I was stalling. "Anyway, he's in ninth grade, and his dad is a pastor. He's not obsessed like Daniel, mind you, he's just nice. And smart. And fun."

"And cute?" Paige asked.

I blushed and nodded. "He has a sister whose name is Kate, like mine. They're coming to dinner in a week or two because they're going to visit relatives in Seattle. After the first tryouts."

That reminded me, I hadn't mentioned the funding issue to them. Maybe I wouldn't. After all, it was going to work out okay. It had to. Working out okay for me, though, meant not working out at all for Paige.

I practiced all weekend. Should I write a new song? I'd worked really hard on that Easter one, though, and I didn't think I could just come up with a new one right away.

"Get outside for a while," my mom said on Saturday after I'd been singing for an hour. She was right. My voice needed a rest.

I tugged a sweater over my head and smoothed the static out of my hair so I didn't look like a mad scientist. Outside, I raked the rest of the leaves that had fallen, then stood looking up at the sky beneath the interlocked fingers of the newly naked trees, branches shivering. I noticed that the next-door neighbors had tons of leaves on their yard. Why not?

I grabbed my rake and gloves and headed over. As soon as I'd made a nice big pile, the twins who lived there came racing out of the house.

"Hooray for Kate!" Lee said as he dived into the pile and tossed leaves all over himself like Uncle Scrooge in a Donald Duck money pit. His sister Nancy looked at me, forlorn.

"I'm sorry," she said. "He just messed up all of your leaves."

I'd been thinking the same thing, but seeing her little face crumple like one of the leaves changed my thoughts. "Let's show him how to really enjoy himself," I said. We raked up our own pile and had a leaf fight.

Leaves stuck in Nancy's hair like tipsy ribbons and on my clothes like silk appliqués. As soon as we started our war, her brother joined us.

"We wuv you, " Lee said.

"I wuv you, too, Lee," I said, mussing his hair. "I wuv you, Nancy."

Soon enough their mom came out. "Which ones are the kindergartners?" she teased. We all laughed and she scooted them back inside to bathe. I raked a few more piles—it was up to their dad what they'd do with them next—and went home.

"You had a call," my dad said when I walked into the house. Saturdays were days off at Rainmaker, but he was hard at work on his sermon for tomorrow. Philippians. I kissed his cheek.

"From who?"

"Paige. She sounded distressed."

I ran into the kitchen and dialed. "Hello, may I speak with Paige?"

"It's me," she said. "I can't go to the tryouts on Monday."

"*What?* Why not?"

"My sister has a college visit, and my mom will be there with her. My dad is on a trip to Seattle for Rainmaker, and my brother has football."

"But you don't have to be at any of those, right?"

"I have no ride." I heard the panic and sorrow in her voice, hidden to those not familiar with tone and meaning. It kind of sounded like a bird flying solo, its flock way ahead on the migration south, not aware that a member was lagging behind, calling out for them to wait up.

I could just tell her I was sorry and save our friendship. If we weren't competing against one another, we wouldn't have to worry about it coming between us. She hadn't even told me what she needed the money from the contest for, so who even knew if it was important? She seemed to have plenty.

Or I could ask my mom if we could pick her up and take her with us. "I'll call you right back," I said.

"Why?" Paige said.

"Just because."

My mom was reading. "Mom? Can we pick up Paige

on Monday and take her to and from the tryouts? Her family is going to be gone."

Mom nodded. "No problem."

I hugged her and went back to the kitchen and called Paige. "We'll come and get you if it's okay with your parents."

"When? On Monday? You'll have to come all the way to Lewiston and get me and then back to Clarkston and then back to Lewiston. It's way out of your way."

"It's okay, we don't mind," I said. We really didn't mind. "We'll drop my dad off a little early and then come and get you." For some reason, even though I knew I *had* to win, I wanted her to have a chance, too. Like with the river we'd walked by, I sensed deep things churning inside her that we hadn't talked about yet.

"Thanks," she said. She didn't really sound glad. I wondered why.

∼

We three left right after school Monday. I didn't want to be late. I knew Paige didn't, either. My mom turned the car off in Paige's driveway while I went up to get her. They had a big pillar with a light in it at the end of their driveway, which was paved. An old lady with a kitten in her arms waved to me from the next yard over. Sweet. I waved back.

"Come in!" Paige dragged me into her house. It was big and full of windows and drapes that looked like prom-gown material, but not gaudy. I was glad my mom had waited in the car. Didn't both of our dads work for Rainmaker? Weren't they both Christians? Why did one have so much and one so little?

"Close your eyes," she said and led me by the hand up to her room. When I got there I saw the cutest, fuzziest little dog sitting on the bed wagging her tail at me.

"It's Brie!" she said. I walked over and sat on the bed. The dog licked my hand and put her tiny head on my leg. Slowly I reached over and petted her silky fur. My heart melted. I'd thought all little dogs were yappy. Till now.

"Cool room," I said. It was all in order, too. Paige opened her closet. "What are those?" I pointed to a two-foot-high stack of coil-bound notebooks in the corner.

"Nothing." Paige dropped a towel over the top of them.

"I love that red sweater." I pointed to the sweater folded on the shelf of her open armoire, suddenly very conscious that my clothes weren't really up to par. I held it up to myself and looked for her approval.

Paige looked stricken. She didn't say anything at all. Was she mad? Had I said something wrong?

"Thanks," she stuttered. "I was just going to put it on."

Funny. She had army green pants on and she looked ready to go. The red sweater wouldn't match that. She'd have to change her whole outfit.

I sat in her room and patted her little dog while she ran into the bathroom and changed.

"Ready," she said, slightly less enthusiastic than she had been before.

"I could get used to a dog like this," I said. "And my mom wouldn't be able to complain about a big mutt taking up half of our house."

Paige smiled. We walked to the car.

"Here, Mrs. Kennedy," Paige said. She handed a folded bill to my mom. "My mom said to please give this to you for gas."

My mom tried to push it away, but Paige insisted. "Please take it. It's the least we can do."

My mom took the bill. "It's no trouble at all, of course," she said. I know she took it to please Paige, but it pained me. We could afford to drive a friend if we wanted.

I let it go. We sat in the backseat together and compared notes. I read her song. It was awesome. Better than the Easter song, I thought. We warmed up our voices together. Mostly, when we sang, she naturally fell into harmonizing with me instead of leading herself.

We were both nervous when we pulled up at the high school. Paige's hand trembled, and I felt sweat trickle down my back. "Want to pray together?" I asked when we sat down. She nodded. I prayed out loud and she just said amen. I don't think she got to lead prayer very often in her house. After praying, we sat together quietly.

"Welcome." The artistic director finally came into the hall and greeted us. I recognized him; he'd helped with the start-up of the Web site, too. I know he taught at the high school and was always looking for ways to get his faith into the school where he could.

"Each contestant will come into the back room, hand his or her song to us—and you have put your names and phone numbers on them, correct?—and then sing 'The Star-Spangled Banner.' We'll let you know who the final contenders are by the end of the week. We'll also let you know exactly what the final round of tryouts will consist of."

We went in alphabetical order, which meant that I went about halfway through, with Kennedy, and Paige went almost last, with Winsome.

"Miss Kennedy?" They called me into the room. There were three people—two women and the high school teacher I had recognized.

"Do I know you?" he asked.

"Yes, I know Moira. I was around when she set up the Web site," I answered.

"How is she doing?" he said, warmth filling his face. "She was such a good student and set a great example for others."

"She's doing fine, I think," I answered. We really

hadn't kept in touch since she started college, even though we'd been good friends at church. She'd led the high school praise band sometimes.

"Well, Miss Kennedy, let's begin." A businesslike woman held out her hand, and I handed my music to her. She gave me a note on the piano and then I was to sing. A cappella. No musical accompaniment.

I closed my eyes and sang, no microphone. I hit every note; I knew it. You know when you're on your game, and I was on my game that afternoon.

When I opened my eyes, the room was quiet. They nodded. The businesslike woman dabbed her eye and quietly said, "Thank you. We'll be in touch."

The guy hurried to open the door for me. *Thank you, Lord,* I said. I didn't say it out loud, though. I didn't want Paige to hear.

A few contestants later the lady called out, "Miss Winsome?"

Most of the contestants had left the waiting area after they tried out, but I waited inside for Paige. I could hear her through the door. I wondered if she'd been able to hear me. I'm sure she could. I sing louder, and I could clearly hear her. She was totally on key but still didn't sound as strong as a soloist should. I felt sick in my gut. The guy opened the door for her, too. Was he just as quick on his feet as he was when I had tried out? Did that lady wipe her eyes for Paige, too? I wasn't sure what

I wanted the answer to be for either question if I'd had a choice.

Paige came out.

"They'll call the finalists," she said as we walked back to the car.

How did she feel about her performance? I wondered. She didn't say and I didn't ask. She didn't ask me, either. Maybe we were trying to protect our friendship. Paige's hands weren't trembling anymore. My sweat had dried up, too. I looked at her out of the corner of my eye and she was looking at me, too. I smiled and she smiled back.

Even if we both made the first cut, we couldn't both win in the end.

CHAPTER FIVE
lewiston, idaho

paige

Even if we both made the first cut, we couldn't both win in the end.

I brought my homework with me baby-sitting a few nights later and tried to get my mind off of that fact. I tried to forget about it a lot that week as we waited to hear back and as Kate and I spent more time on the phone, on email, and in person getting to know each other.

I learned that she has always wanted a cat but is afraid of the expense. I'd fix that if I could. I *would* fix the elderly people up with a pet for life—people who had nobody and pets who were going to be put to sleep otherwise. Young pets who needed a chance to live, with old people who needed something to live for. It was clear to me that Kate had lots of people to love her. She was the first truly popular person I liked, and in some ways it was changing my feelings about all populars.

The committee would call us tomorrow.

"I'll be there in a second," I called up to Valerie, the little girl I was baby-sitting. I didn't baby-sit very often, and time was dragging. Valerie's parents had agreed to take in the hamster from the pet store that I'd nursed back to health, so I'd brought her with me tonight. I'd already set up the cage, got food and water set, and introduced her to her new five-year-old owner. The hamster was ready to go back to bed, and so was I. Valerie and I had already played hide-and-seek. I had no more tricks up my sleeve.

I dialed Clarkston. "Kate," I said as soon as she answered, "quick, give me some baby-sitting ideas. I need help and you know kids!"

"How about a water balloon toss in the back-yard?"

"Great, if I had a bunch of water balloons stuck in my back pocket."

We both laughed. "Get a piece of paper," she said.

"PAAAAIGE," Valerie called from upstairs. "Is the hamster supposed to be doing this?"

Uh-oh!

I grabbed the closest thing at hand, a napkin, and jotted down the ideas as Kate spouted.

Coloring. Drawing. Okay, I could do that. We could doodle. Sing-alongs. "Now, why didn't I think of that?"

" 'Cause I have experience," Kate said.

"No, 'cause you're the kid person," I said. "And I'm not. If Valerie barked or meowed, I'd know what to do."

"You'll be a kid person, too, with experience," she said. "We still on for a walk by the river after school tomorrow and swimming on Saturday?"

"If I can get rides," I said. I was *not* going to have her mom pick me up again like I was an orphan. No way. Even though I really wanted to go. That was so embarrassing. "See you," I said before she could offer.

"Okay," she said. I could hear the puzzlement in her voice. I didn't know if we were at that level of friendship though. I hadn't told her how I was low Joe at my house.

I raced upstairs. The hamster had pulled her plastic bed from the top shelf to the bottom shelf and was caving in there like a soldier under siege. Valerie was poking a food stick at her.

"Here," I said. "Let me teach you how to do this."

We closed the bedroom door and opened the cage.

"She's not going to like me, only you," Valerie said. She began crying. "I never had a pet. They don't like me." Panic rose in my chest, but I willed it down.

"She will," I promised. "Let's try this." I cupped my hand over Valerie's, and slowly we reached in and scooped the hamster into our hands. Then we slowly withdrew.

"She won't bite me, will she?"

"She's never bitten anyone yet."

As we sat on the floor, Valerie took the hamster in her own dimpled hands and petted the top of her silky head with a tiny pointer finger. The hamster stretched out and relaxed. Valerie laughed. "She likes me! She likes me!"

I smiled. Putting people and pets together was something I was growing to love. "What are you going to name her?" I asked as Valerie cuddled her pet before putting the contented hamster back into her home.

Please don't let it be something like Clouds or Diamond, I thought, knowing the names little girls favored, but knowing, too, that I had named my kitten Sparkle when I was a small girl.

"Cinnamon," Valerie answered.

I gently tugged her pigtail in agreement. "Good

choice! You're going to be a very good pet owner, Valerie." I stood up. "Let's go downstairs and draw."

Valerie made thumbprint people out of ink and pencil. I doodled a kindly princess coddling a happy hamster.

When her dad drove me home a few hours later, I had earned twenty dollars for baby-sitting and ten dollars for the hamster—which I'd gotten for free, since she'd been bitten at the pet store. I took the money, though, knowing that it would allow me to care for another pet until it could be placed. Or go toward the four hundred dollars I needed for the pet program.

Had I been absolutely crazy to sign up for that program without having the money? Cold fear crept up my spine. But wasn't that what faith was all about? Stepping out when you didn't know? A little voice inside me wondered if that was maybe just taking advantage of God's goodness to fix whatever wreck you caused when you drove your life into a telephone pole.

When I got home, everyone was in his or her room except my mom, who was sitting by the fireplace, quietly. My mom is never quiet.

"Everything okay?" I asked.

"Oh . . . yes. How did baby-sitting go?"

"I made thirty dollars. Even better, I taught Valerie how to care for a pet."

My mom looked up. She cupped her hand around the mug on the table in front of her, the tea tag draping out of it like a forgotten price ticket. "That's more important to you than the money, isn't it?"

"It is," I agreed. "They told me at the shelter that when I am sixteen I'll be able to work there after school and on weekends."

My mom looked up, slightly shocked. "You're planning pretty far ahead," she said. "We don't know what the future holds in two years."

That was weird. My mom never talked like that.

I yawned. "Can you drive me to meet Kate at the Riverwalk after school tomorrow?"

"Yes," my mom said. She didn't even add a comment like, "And after that I'll have twenty errands to run."

"Should I wait for Dad at the office, then, and he can take me home?"

"Yes," Mom said. As soon as I mentioned his office, I saw her eyes flicker. "Paige, you don't have plans for next weekend, do you?"

"Nooo. This weekend I'm going swimming at the teen dip, but nothing next weekend. Kate and I thought we might go to the mall. Why?"

"Dad's taking us all to Walla Walla. Can the mall wait?"

A vacation? To Walla Walla of all places? "Sure. Why are we going?"

"Oh, he's got some meeting to go to and wants us all to spend time together." She stood up and said nothing more.

Mom came and kissed me, ending the conversation. "Love you. See you tomorrow morning."

I ran upstairs and emailed Kate that our walk was on. Then I started folding my clothes. When I got to the red sweater, I sat down on my bed with it in my hands.

I'm so ashamed, I said to God. I saw how Kate had looked at that sweater. I should have offered it. Truly, it would have looked really good on her. I mean, I wasn't planning to wear it to the first tryouts. I'd wanted to feel so good and have an edge, so I ran into the bathroom looking like a total fool and changed at the last minute.

I looked at it, the soft yarn limp in my hands. I didn't even like it anymore. The verse I'd shouted to Janie came back at me. *"All the believers were of one heart and mind, and they felt that what they owned was not their own; they shared everything they had."*

I couldn't even loan it to her now, knowing I'd be giving her second best. It wasn't right. It's because she sang so well. *She sings better than I do,* I admitted to myself. Better than Mallory. Better than any girl I've ever known. So I hadn't been ready to let her

have my red sweater. I threw it toward the bottom of
my bed, where I wouldn't have to stare at it all day.

The next morning my mom was up early making
high-cholesterol omelets for everyone. On a school
day. Weird.

Walter was waiting at my locker.

"How was soccer?" I asked politely. Right then
and there I decided that whomever I married had to
eat vegetarian Chinese food—that is, not be afraid of
what other people think—and never, ever play soccer.

"Good," he said. "Did you hear about the tryouts?"

I looked at him sharply. "How did you know
about that?"

"Your brother told the football team. It got back
to me through Jack's sister, who knows my sister."

I closed the locker and slid the lock into place. It
was going to be just like sports tryouts all over again.

"No, I haven't heard," I said. He looked so earnest
that I softened. "I should hear today. I'll email you.
Thanks for asking."

He smiled. "Lots of us are rooting for you, you know. We want you to win."

I chucked him on the arm. "Thanks," I said. On the way to class, I let it sink in. Other people were hopeful for me, too. I wasn't the only overlooked person in the universe. It made me doubly sure I had to win. I'd try hard. I'd pray hard. And God was on my side and theirs.

After school my mom picked me up so we could go right to the Riverwalk. "You got a phone call," she said.

"What did it say?"

She handed her cell phone to me. "Call the voice mail and listen for yourself."

I could barely hold down the hotkey to connect to voice mail.

"Hello, this is the Worship Works team. We'd like to let Miss Paige Winsome know that she is one of the top five contestants. Final tryouts will be in less than two weeks; exact date and time will be mailed to you. You'll need to submit and perform a new composition, something you haven't shared before, written by you alone. Please prepare an additional song to sing, as well. Congratulations, Miss Winsome."

"Hey! I got it!" I shouted.

"You made the first round, anyway," Mom said. "That's great." I felt my face drop and saw that she knew immediately that was the wrong thing to say.

"I'm sorry. I didn't mean to spoil your joy," she said.

I didn't say anything. Was that how she responded to Justin's football games? Well, you won this one, but don't count on the next one? Or Janie's college admittance? Great, you got into Idaho State, but don't count on Whitman? No, I didn't think so.

I turned my back to her.

"I'm sorry," she said again. I was sorry, too.

I let her kiss my cheek as she dropped me off at the Riverwalk. My chest felt tight and sad. I wanted to burrow into the ground and hide like a worm.

"Hi." Kate was already there since her dad had to be at work early.

"Hi," I said. She looked at me. I know she could see I was sad. She was probably worried I hadn't made it. But then—she hadn't said anything, either. Which of us was going to bring it up?

"How was your day?" she asked. Was she fishing?

"Good," I said. The cool air against my skin refreshed me some. "How about you?"

"Good," she answered. I'm glad she was brave, because she went next and I just wasn't up for it after the tiff with my mom. "Did you hear back from Worship Works?" Her voice was gentle.

"Yes—I made it." I looked at her face.

She smiled. "Me too!" She grabbed my hands and

we jumped up and down like we were Valerie's age.

We picked up the pace now. "It's *so* cool that we both made it," she said. "I was hoping we'd either both make it or both not."

I nodded. "I've got to find another song to sing," I said. "As for the composition, I have some in my journal, and then there's the new one, though I have some . . . questions about that. What to do with it, I mean," I said. I wasn't sure it would be ready in time. It might be. I was mighty glad I hadn't burned my journals. They had one more chance to be worthy.

"I've got the opposite problem," she said. "I have lots of good songs prepared to sing, especially since we're doing new songs on the praise team in church."

I was silent. She didn't know how painful that was for me. If I'd been on the praise team, I'd probably have a few good new songs ready, too. I hoped with all my might that I won and that Mallory and Britt would be at the game. Then I looked back at Kate and remembered that if I won she lost.

"How about composition?" I tried to change the subject.

"Hmm, not sure," she said. "The Easter song was my best—only—song."

"Let's get together and talk about it some more later," I said. We'd reached the end of the Riverwalk.

"You still on for the pool?" I asked.

She shook her head. "My dad has a meeting at the

church on Saturday afternoon, and my mom has to be there with him. Finances."

"Well, *we* can drive you," I said. "Why not? You took me?"

Kate looked uncomfortable. "I don't know."

"Please," I said. I decided to open up to her. I just felt like it was time to see if we could go to a new level of trust. You never know what might happen when you do that with a new friend. They could think you're totally weird and trying to rush the friendship, or they could hurt you. But I wanted to try. I didn't think Kate would hurt me.

"Since my friend Maddie moved to Hawaii, I haven't really had a friend that I had so much in common with. I mean, I do have friends." I didn't want her to think I was a total reject. "But you just can't make it be like you have a lot of stuff in common with people you really don't. It would be fun to have you there."

"Will Walter be there?" She looked at me slyly.

"Probably, but Walter is *not* potential boyfriend material. Seriously. Unless you're interested."

"No way!" she teased. "I just wanted to have some fun." She looked at me. "Okay, if you say so. Other people come, not just from your church, right?"

"Right," I said. "And it's free."

I thought I saw her flinch when I said that. I just meant to reassure her, but something went wrong.

We walked back to the office, and my dad drove me home.

When we got home, I went right to my room. I saw the red sweater still crumpled at the foot of the bed and thought about how selfish I had been with someone I really cared about. Kate. I knew my mom was up the hall. Even moms make mistakes. I went into her room and hugged her and she hugged me back, not even carrying one speck of a grudge. "I love you and I'm sorry," I said.

"I know," she answered. "I'm not the most sensitive person in the world sometimes. I need to slow down and think. I'm working on it. I'm sorry, too."

I stared in amazement. That was the first time I'd ever heard my mom say she was working on something inside.

All was right with the world. Till Saturday, anyway.

The Turkey Bowl would be played in Clarkston, where Kate lives. It's a smaller town than Lewiston and has less money, although nice people don't mention that. The houses are prettier in some ways, though, because rather than being all new and just having that flat, Astroturf lawn that lots of our developments have, their lawns are sculpted. They look like birthday cakes—bunches of flowers cascading everywhere, even in the fall. As we drove to pick up Kate, I noticed some of the flowers were frozen—

they would be brown by next month, but they still looked pretty scaling the old houses.

I wasn't prepared for Kate's house. It was really small. But it had vines growing around the trees and across the roof ledges like a little cottage set in England. It had character. I'd have to tell her that. She ran out as soon as she saw our car driving up.

"Hello," she said, climbing into the backseat. She reached forward and handed a folded bill to my dad. "This is for gas." I could see he was about to decline taking it, but I gave him a really hard stare before I got out of the front and joined her in the back.

"Thanks," he said and slipped it into the ashtray. Whew. He'd got the signal.

We drove back to Lewiston and to the pool. Lots of people from the junior high group were already there in the party room, bathing suits and cover-ups on while they munched pizza.

When I walked into the room with Kate, everyone got silent. Mallory walked over to say hello. Do people like her have a sensor or something that lets them know that someone of status has entered the room?

"Introduce us to your friend," she said. Britt dogged along behind her.

"This is Kate. She lives in Clarkston," I said.

"Hi," Kate said. "Thanks for allowing guests."

"You're welcome. You can come and sit with us if

you want." Mallory pointed to the section she and Britt had marked off in the party room.

"Oh, thanks, but I think Paige and I wanted to swim right away," Kate said. I smiled.

A couple other guys from youth group and a girl I didn't know were already in the pool. Walter joined us and introduced the girl as Hayley.

"Do you go to our church?" I asked. "It's a big place; it's hard to know everyone."

"I do," she answered.

"Have you been to youth group?"

"No," she admitted, then added softly enough so only I could hear, "I didn't feel very comfortable there."

I smiled. "I know how you feel. Well, if you come next week, look for me." She smiled back.

The six of us played a game of Marco Polo and then ate pizza together in our own circle.

"I hear you're trying out to sing for the Turkey Bowl—I hope you win!" Hayley said to me.

Uh-oh.

"Well, I'm sure you'll do better than anyone else," Walter said. Ouch! Ouch! I couldn't listen anymore. I needed to say something before Kate felt bad. I looked at her, and she caught my eye. She shook her head no. I said nothing.

We swam some more and had a great time.

"Ever notice the sounds of music around you?" Kate asked.

I smiled. "Like the drops in the pool, the swish of the towels?"

"The snap of the chairs and the creaks going on around you in the bleachers," she added.

"Non-musical people would think we are weird."

"We *are* weird," she said. We laughed together.

Afterward, as we got changed in the dressing room, Kate said, "Have you found a song to sing for the contest yet?"

"Nope. I usually sing harmony, so I have to look for a lead."

"I noticed that," she said. She looked up at me. "Nothing bad, I just noticed that you harmonized a lot. I thought maybe it was because you weren't used to singing lead—or might not feel comfortable with that yet."

Well! Maybe this is how popular pastors' daughters think.

"I'm totally comfortable singing lead, thanks," I said.

"You don't have to get huffy," she said. "It's not like I said you were a weak singer." Then she shut her mouth quickly.

So! She thinks I'm a weak singer. Before I could help myself, I asked her, "Have you written a new song yet?"

She knew it was a zap. "Nope. I'm sure I will, though. It can't be that hard."

I felt my face flush and saw that hers was in high color, too. And it wasn't from steam off of the pool.

My dad drove us home in silence. He was too wrapped up in his own worries to say much. After we dropped Kate off, I took out a notepad and doodled so I wouldn't have to talk. I drew a tired terrier in slippers sleeping in front of a fireplace. I drew a pit bull at a pool. Then I stopped.

When we got home, I threw myself on my bed and cried. I had trusted her! I had told her that I hadn't had a good friend since Maddie. She had seemed so right—so perfect, even knowing what to say to Mallory and Britt.

Lord, I pleaded, *what went wrong?*

CHAPTER SIX
clarkston, washington

kate

What went wrong? I asked myself that on the way home in the car, and I asked God, too, in my heart.

I planned to call Paige as soon as I got home since we couldn't very well talk in front of her dad. Then I got home and talked with Mom.

"Maybe it's better to cool off a little," Mom said. "Why don't you think through what you really mean, and what you meant then? Is it possible that you do think you're better than she is?"

"No," I said. I popped a brownie into my mouth, chewed, and swallowed it practically without tasting.

I didn't watch a movie with my mom and dad that night. Paige didn't call, either.

Three days went by with no word. Wednesday I got up early and had breakfast with my mom and dad like we always did. Since we don't get to eat dinner together every night, we always eat breakfast together.

"How are things between you and your new friend?" Dad asked. My mom kept her eyes on the griddle, so I knew she had told him about my fight with Paige.

"Okay," I said. "And I don't really think I'm better than she is. Although maybe I have a little more experience as a lead singer."

"Hmm," Dad said. That was all. "Hmm." After a minute of silence he spoke up again.

"Do you think that what you have is of yourself and not from God, whether it's money or talent?"

I shook my head, ate my waffle, and talked normally so they wouldn't see how upset I was. I did leave early to walk to school in hopes that the cool air would help clear my head. What Dad asked bugged me more than I let on. I was *not* like Mrs. Doyle, being holier than thou and acting like what I had was better than what other people had. Right?

"See you later!" Lee and Nancy called out at their bus

stop. I waved back, tickled. They were already looking forward to my baby-sitting tonight.

Maybe I had been self-righteous. Maybe I did think I was better. Lead singing was the only thing I had to hang on to sometimes. Because in my world, where everything to hold on to to feel safe was topsy-turvy, music was the only thing I always knew was mine and couldn't be taken away.

"Hold on to *me*." I felt the voice in my heart. I knew who that was.

I kicked a leaf and it cartwheeled across the street. Part of me didn't want to unclench my fist and trust. Part of me longed to believe Jesus would hold on to me no matter what. Part of me worried He wouldn't.

I mucked through the day and got home and placed a call to Paige. "Hi," I said. "I was wondering if you wanted to come over tomorrow night," I said. "I understand if you're busy or something."

She laughed and I felt carefree again, like Lee and Nancy in the leaves. "Did you get my email?" she asked.

"Nope."

"I just emailed to see if you wanted to get together again before the weekend. I know you're having *special* company, and we're going to Walla Walla soon."

I grinned. She was talking about Kyle, of course. "I really would like to get together," I said. "Do you want to come over here tomorrow?"

"Yeah. I'm glad you called. I'll see you tomorrow—if my mom can take me."

By then I knew not to suggest picking her up. She wanted me to see her mom as a mom who cared. Actually, I did see her mom as one who cared. Paige just needed to feel that for herself.

That night I skipped youth group for the first time all year.

"Why did you agree to baby-sit?" my mom asked. I was going next door to sit with the twins while their mom went to sell some of her handwork at a craft show.

"She called at the last minute. It was an emergency."

There was more to it, and my mom knew it. She would let me unravel the story in my own time, though, and now was not the time. Maybe later.

I trudged across the cold ground, through my yard and over to the neighbors'. Lee opened the door wearing a slightly small worn-out Superman cape. I knew his mom had scored it at Goodwill. She'd told me so.

"Hey, Kate's here!" Lee jumped on my back and Nancy tugged at my hand.

"Give her some space," their mom said. She pointed to the fridge. "There's the number where I'll be if you need me. It was very generous of you to come at the last minute."

I got that creepy feeling when someone gave me credit for something I didn't really do—not dishonest, actually, but maybe just a little unclean, like the thin sheet of film on unbrushed teeth had stretched over my soul.

We went outside and raked the few stray leaves.

"Not enough to jump into." Lee shook his head. "What else can we do?"

I looked around and noticed the gnarled apple tree in my backyard, kind of where our yards were stitched together. I hadn't picked apples in years. We just kind of let them fall to the ground as a bonus for the squirrels.

"Want to pick apples?"

"Yeah!" Nancy said. We ran over to my garage and got a big box and then headed back over to the grandfatherly tree. "Hey, look at this one!" I held up a puckered, dented apple. "It looks like an old man's face."

Nancy looked distressed. "I want to find one with a pretty face."

We picked and crunched and finally found one with a pretty face. Actually, I thought it was puckered, too, but Nancy didn't, so it was a go.

Their mom came home an hour after they were in bed. I'd been sitting there thinking about how to make more money. Kyle and his family were coming Friday night. I knew they'd want to make plans for the Wee Care kids' Christmas program. Maybe I could baby-sit and earn enough money to pay for a small gift in case I lost the contest. But then the kids would have little trinkets— again. I wanted them to have something fabulous. Just once. One year. One time. One Christmas.

"Thank you," I said as I folded the money I'd just earned into my hand. "I was wondering if you know of anyone else who needs a baby-sitter—maybe the people on the other side of you?" I pointed to their other next-door neighbors.

"I don't know, but they asked about you," she answered. "I mentioned that you were baby-sitting tonight, and she asked if I'd send you over for something. I don't think it was baby-sitting, though." She checked her watch. "Probably too late. Maybe they *do* want a baby-sitter. I think they're moving, though, so it wouldn't be steady work."

I didn't need steady work, just some money to get me to December.

When I got home, my mom was up reading my dad's sermon notes. "How'd it go?" she asked.

"Great," I said. "She said those people on the other side of them might want me for a baby-sitter, too. I'll go over there tomorrow. Remember, Paige is coming over, too."

"Would you like me to make something special for her dinner with us?" my mom asked.

"She likes Chinese food a lot." I wanted it to be really nice. "And she's a vegetarian."

"Okay, I'll look through my lengthy collection of vege-tarian Chinese recipes," my mom teased. I knew she'd find something good even though we were going to be stretched by making dinner for our visitors on Friday night, too.

I read over my dad's sermon notes, since they were just sitting there, while I ate an apple. Dad always printed the verse at the top of the page to keep himself focused.

Let nothing be done through selfish ambition or conceit, but in lowliness of mind let each esteem others better than himself. Let each of you look out not only for his own interests, but also for the interests of others. Philippians 2:3–4

I set the page down and went into my mom's room. "You know why I didn't go tonight?"

Mom patted the bed beside her. She was brushing out her hair, earrings twinkling. "Tell me."

"Because I thought the right thing to do would be to give Vickie a chance to lead music."

"Why didn't you just go and give her a turn, then?"

"I guess I'm willing to let her have a turn but not willing to give it to her."

My mom kissed my forehead. "I'm proud of you," she said. If it were my daughter, I wouldn't be proud of me. I kissed her back, then went to my room and crawled into bed. I lay awake wondering if things would be weird between Paige and me. The first fight always tests a new friendship.

The next afternoon we got home just before Paige arrived. Personally, I thought it was silly because we had just been in Lewiston to drop my dad off at work and could have picked her up. The thing about Paige is, she doesn't talk a lot, but if you listen with your heart you know what she wants and what she doesn't. I wondered if she'd think my house was tiny and weird. She'd never been inside.

"Hi," she said. She had brought her—my—guitar with her. Right then I realized that part of me would always be with her; part of my music would always be with her and hers with me. I don't know if she realized that and that's why she brought it, or if God just put that in my head.

"Come on in my room," I said. She hauled the guitar and a bag in with her. I couldn't help being curious. What was in the bag?

We went into the room and she handed the bag to me. It felt squishy. I knew it was clothes. A picture of Mrs. Doyle flashed before me.

"Clothes?" I said. I knew my voice sounded mad, and I reminded myself—*Don't say anything you'll regret.*

"Yeah," Paige answered. She looked confused. "My sister always shares her clothes with her best friends. I, um, just thought you might want to borrow this for your dinner tomorrow night. If you don't want to, though, it's okay."

I opened the bag to find the red sweater I had loved.

"I've worn the sweater," she said sadly.

Why was she sad? As if I had expected her not to wear her own clothes? "But the bracelet is new. I wanted you to wear it first."

I can be so stupid. Here my new friend, who had just called me one of her *best* friends, was sharing her clothes, and I was all huffy over our little spat.

I'm sorry, Lord, I said. *I see where I've been going wrong. Fix me.* I smiled to myself. *I need to be tuned.*

When Paige saw me smile, she smiled, too. "What are you smiling about?"

"First of all, because I really love this outfit and will totally wear it tomorrow night when Kyle comes," I said. "Second, because I feel so bad that I had a rude attitude toward you. I was mean and self-righteous about singing lead. So when I was praying about it, I felt like I needed to be tuned, you know, like a basically good instrument that got off-key."

She laughed with me. "That's something I can totally understand. I was rude, too. I knew exactly what to say back that would hurt you, that you were worried about writing music, and I didn't waste any time saying it."

"I have an idea. What if I help you strengthen your vocals and you help me learn how to write music?"

Paige nodded. "Kind of like chopsticks." She twisted

the one in her ponytail. "One alone is only good for being pretty but can't do real work. Two together can work, though."

"You know," I said, "if I help you and you help me, we'll both get better...." I didn't finish the thought but just swallowed my gum.

"And that means one of us is more likely to win, but then it means that's more like one will win and one will lose." The room grew cool and a little darker.

She knew what I was thinking. I nodded. We said nothing else. I'm not sure either of us was ready to commit to more. One of us really would lose. No matter what. She'd told me on the phone once why she needed the money, for the animals and the elderly. I knew that was really important. We could always try to come up with another way to make money, but I knew in my heart that what she really needed wasn't money. She needed her gifts and talents to shine for her family. I needed to help my Nez Perce friends and the little kids who always got the castaway clothes and small presents like I always had. I needed to know God cared and would provide for me without my rigging up a way to bring in the cash again. Just God. For us. Paige understood that. Yet one of us must lose.

After dinner I showed her some more vocal techniques. "See? If you breathe this way and open your nasal passages, the tone comes out more clearly," I said.

"Cool!" she agreed. When she sang again, it was much cleaner and clearer.

"You're a lead!" I laughed.

She showed me some writing techniques. "When you repeat one thought every once in a while, that's the thought people will take away," she explained. "You can say it differently in the refrain than you do in the song itself and still make the point without getting boring."

I did see. I could use this stuff. We wrote a line together that I decided I would definitely keep for my new song.

"I'll email you a song before I leave tomorrow and you can copy the techniques for your new one," she said. "Just use your own words and chords."

That night, when she left, all was right with the world. Till tomorrow, when Kyle and his family would come and ask how the Christmas program was going to be laid out and when we could shop for the presents so they'd be there in time.

Late that night I grabbed my mom's photo albums off of the highest shelf in our living room and took them to my room. Isn't it funny how many pictures people take at Christmas? I mean, if you were an alien or something and you came down to earth and only judged us by our pictures, you'd think every day was a birthday party or a vacation or Christmas.

I stuck a piece of gum into my mouth and chewed as I flipped through page after page. Me as a baby and a toddler when we all lived with Grandma so my dad could finish Bible school.

Me as a kindergartner with missing teeth in front of a Charlie Brown tree cut from the backyard. Even though they said it was special because it was a Charlie Brown tree, I knew it was small. My ornament from preschool had bowed the branch.

Me in elementary school learning the very important lesson that Christmas wasn't about presents but still wishing I could both celebrate Jesus and have the gift of a sister or a brother who wanted to drink from a bottle and wore a real diaper. I closed the book and went to sleep.

The next day we were all humming to get the house ready for company—even my dad had the night off. My mom put her best clothes on, and I could smell pot roast and potatoes and carrots glazing in gravy in her huge slow cooker. At six o'clock that evening they arrived.

I hadn't seen Kyle for a while, but we understood each other. His dad was the pastor of a small church and also had another job breeding horses. We'd grown up bumping into each other at church events, and our moms were friends. I think they were on their way to Seattle tonight after they ate with us. I wondered if Kyle looked the same. I wondered if he thought about me very often.

Mrs. Lapthorn was at the door first. "Welcome!" My mom threw her arms around her friend and ushered her into the house. My dad had already gone outside to meet Pastor Lapthorn at the car.

"Kate!" Katie came running, black braids flying behind her as she leaped into my arms. I picked her up and swung her around. "Set me down!" she commanded. Then she twirled. "Look at my skirt. It whirls when I spin. Kyle says I'm like a princess and that you're going to bring presents for all of us at Christmas. Then we can *all* be princesses for a day. I told all my friends—but I didn't tell them *you* were bringing them. Everyone knows they'll be coming from their moms and dads. You're just helping! You're playing Santa Claus!"

Lightning shot through my chest. The kids were counting on gifts. *Parents* were counting on gifts, and I know the church was using this as an outreach. Well, I had promised after all, hadn't I? I must get them.

Kyle walked up. He'd gotten taller. I knew there was a joke among old people about tall, dark, and handsome. I didn't know if teens were old enough to be considered actually handsome or just cute. Maybe both.

"Hey, Kate." He came up and clapped my arm, then smiled, his eyes crinkling. At that moment he was still cute, but more my great friend of many years. I was comfortable with him again. I'd missed him.

"Hey, Kyle," I said. "Let's go inside."

We followed our parents in, and while the adults chatted in the living room, Kyle, Katie, and I went into the kitchen.

"Can I get you something to drink?" I asked.

"Coke, please," Kyle said. I opened three cans and poured one for each of us into glasses with ice and brought them back to the table.

"Tell me about school," I said to Katie. "I know that you're in kindergarten, right?"

"Well, I'm learning to read. English and Sahaptin. Watch." She traced a few letters on the tablecloth.

"Good job!" I said. She beamed. Kyle grinned at her. I'd known Katie for as long as she had lived with their family. Kyle's family had adopted her as a small child.

"I have lots of friends and we have lots of fun." Katie climbed down from her chair and ran into the next room to ask her mother for a pen and paper to show me some other letters she had learned.

"I was really jealous when your family adopted her," I told Kyle. I adjusted the red bracelet on my arm, hoping he'd notice it. *Thank you, Paige*, I thought to myself. She was such a gift to me already. She knew what would make me feel good on this special night, and she shared.

"Why?"

"You were the only other kid I knew who was an only

child. You had pets—horses—and I had none. Then you were getting a sister, something I'd always wanted. And I couldn't!"

"Ah, she looks up to you, you know that," Kyle said. "And you're welcome to come out and ride the horses anytime. I can show you how when you come for Christmas. I'm looking forward to that."

I twisted the bracelet again so the prettiest beads would catch the light. I said nothing.

"Dinner time," my mom called. Everyone came into the kitchen and sat down at the table. I'm a lefty. Whenever I sit next to a right-handed person, we bump elbows. I couldn't decide if I should try to sit next to Kyle so we'd bump elbows or if that would be totally goofy and obvious. My dad settled it for me.

"Why don't you sit here—between me and Kyle," Dad suggested. He put me next to Kyle—but on his left side. No bumping elbows. I looked at Dad out of the corner of my eye to see if he had done that on purpose. He looked at me with that innocent stare. Too innocent. I blushed.

I sat down and pushed the bracelet back some so it wouldn't clink on the plate.

"Is something wrong with your wrist?" Kyle looked at me with concern.

"I'm sorry, I don't understand," I said. The table, which had just been buzzing like bees with passing plates and conversation, grew as quiet as caterpillars.

"I just wondered if something was wrong with your

wrist, you know, maybe an injury with the guitar or something. You keep rubbing it."

How embarrassing! Far from noticing the beautiful bracelet, he thought I had an injury. "No, no," I muttered. "My wrist is fine." The plate passing resumed.

"Speaking of guitars," Kyle's dad spoke up, "it's so cool that you're going to come to our church and help the kids learn to sing when you bring the gifts for the Wee Care program. The kids will be so excited to get a real gift this year, and the parents are grateful to give a bigger gift for once."

"We know how that feels, don't we?" My mom laughed. "Several years we gave gifts to Kate without having any idea who purchased them for us."

I never knew. Wow. I'd have to go back and look at those albums again.

I swallowed. "Yes, yes, I'm looking forward to it."

"Well, we're going to use it as a community outreach. We're inviting people to church for the program, people we think we can help and love and share the Gospel with. Some people want to come to church on Christmas, when they think God is taking attendance, and then find a reason to really stay. Thank you for helping us out with the Wee Care matching program. It gives us a reason to ask them to come." Pastor Lapthorn speared another potato.

"We've always appreciated the times you've come to help our church," my dad responded.

"It's good for believers to work together," Kyle's mom spoke up. "I understand one of your congregation is sponsoring Kate so she'll have the money to buy the gifts when we come back in December."

Neither of my parents spoke, but they both looked at me. They didn't waver. I knew right then that Mrs. Doyle had already told them I'd said we didn't need her money. Usually I was all about telling them that I was old enough to handle my own business, but at this very moment I wished they'd jump in and rescue me. Were they going to blow my secret?

"It's great the many ways the Lord provides." I hoped that wasn't a lie. I didn't say that Mrs. Doyle *was* or *was not* going to give the money. Just that the Lord would provide.

"Well, we're sure looking forward to it. You're going to come and stay a few days, aren't you?" Kyle's mom turned back to my mother. The heat was off of me. For now.

I'm sorry, God, I said inside, the bracelet suddenly heavy. I let it clink against the plate. I had done whatever I wanted and expected Him to pick up the pieces of my mess, expecting him to put Humpty Dumpty back together again.

"How is your job?" Kyle's dad asked my dad.

"Not good," Dad admitted. "I don't know how long we can keep going. I just hope we don't lose our jobs before Christmas."

I had had no idea it was *that* bad.

"I've heard that our operating manager is going to Walla Walla this weekend for a last-ditch effort to find a buyer, someone already invested in Washington and Idaho farming. No one else was interested. But they already have a plant. So whether they want to expand or not—I don't know."

Operating manager? Paige's dad!

"Times are tough," Pastor Lapthorn agreed.

When dinner was over, Kyle and Katie and I cleared the table. Then we went out into the backyard, where my dad had started our fire pit. Katie grabbed a bag of marshmallows and the bouquet of twigs we had whittled from our trees. My mom and Mrs. Lapthorn each balanced a small stack of blankets, like pancakes resting lazily one on another, and brought them out. I got the new guitar. The one the Doyles had given me.

This time my dad didn't direct the seating arrangement. We each chose where we wanted to sit. Kyle sat next to me, on my left. I grinned and he grinned back. His mom sat on my other side because she sang so beautifully and we often sang together.

"Kate has entered a contest—a singing and songwriting contest. When she wins, she not only gets money but also gets to sing at half time at the Thanksgiving Day Turkey Bowl at the high school."

"Wow, you'll be famous," Katie said.

"I don't even know if I'll win." I tweaked her cheek.

"You'll win," Kyle said. "I wish I could be there to see it."

We sang old favorites, like "Come Let Us Worship the Lord," and fun ones like "I'm a Believer." We finally ended with "Heart of Worship."

What was *my* heart of worship? My dad's disturbing comments from earlier—about thinking my gifts were mine, not God's—came back to me, unwanted.

Then it was time for them to get on the road if they were going to get to Seattle that night. I knew they'd get there really late, but I also knew they didn't mind. That's what friends are for.

I set the guitar down and we walked them to the door. I was quiet; so were they. It was a good quiet, though.

We gave everyone a hug good-bye. I tried not to feel too weird hugging Kyle, but if I didn't hug him, that would seem even more weird. Was that my dad watching?

"See you at Christmas," Katie said as she kissed my cheek, "when you bring presents for my friends. I will make a present for you. And for Jesus."

I tugged her braid.

Kyle smiled, and I remembered again how much older he looked. "Thanks for everything you're doing. For our church. For the Lord. For Katie," he said. "For me. See you at Christmas." Kyle turned back once before he left. "You'll win."

We closed the door after waving to them as they drove away.

I washed the dishes slowly. I put them away slowly. The windowpanes were glassy with the cold of November that was knocking at the door. My hands felt cold, too. I finished the dishes and walked into the living room.

"I have something to say," I said. Neither parent looked surprised.

"I told Mrs. Doyle I didn't need her money," I said. "Now I feel just sick." I turned to my mother. "I also told her you didn't need the stupid garbage bag of clothing she had made for you."

"You have no right to speak for me," Mom said. Her tone was gentle, but she didn't hold back on the words.

"I know."

"You didn't really have a right to say no to the gifts for the kids, either," Dad said. "You made a promise."

"I know." I hung my head. "She's just so mean. She makes me feel so small. I'm tired of having people give us stuff all the time. Why can't *God* just give us the stuff instead of *her*?"

Dad put his arm around me. "So what are you going to do now?"

"I could ask for the clothes bag back," I said, turning toward my mother.

Mom shook her head. "I have enough clothes." My heart sank. It wasn't really true. At least from my perspective.

"I am going to win the contest. I can spend the money on the kids. I know I can win. I prayed about it and felt peaceful about it and certain. It's one way I can do it on my own. God understands that."

My parents didn't say anything. Sometimes I wished they were more like those problem-solving parents instead of just *sitting*. Mom got up. "I'm going to get my slippers and some ointment for my hands. Why don't you two pick a movie?"

"I'll pray with you, Kate," Dad said. "And brainstorm, if you want. But you have to figure this one out for yourself. It might mean going back to Mrs. Doyle to ask for the money. It might mean telling the Lapthorns there won't be presents."

I shook my head. "I can win."

Dad smiled. "So," he said, "what movie will it be tonight?"

"I don't know," I said.

"Anything but *Kiss Me, Kate*." I saw the mischief in his eyes as he named an old movie my mom enjoyed.

"Dad!" I said. The last person you want to notice or know about any crush is your *dad*!

I looked around. "Here." If he could play that game, so could I. I'd picked *Fiddler on the Roof,* about a Russian Jewish matchmaker, out of our collection of garage-sale movie finds.

My dad and I giggled together till we burst out laughing.

The movie was great. But I couldn't help remembering Kyle's last words and what it really meant about him and me and the Lord and the contest and Mrs. Doyle and the gifts.

"See you at Christmas," he'd said.

"You'll win."

CHAPTER SEVEN
walla walla, washington

paige

"You'll win." Two important guys in my life would say that in the course of one weekend.

"So—what can I borrow?" It was Friday afternoon, the day after I'd been at Kate's. I plopped down on Janie's wonderful wrought-iron bed.

"What do you mean, what can you borrow?" Janie had a department store's worth of clothes laid out. She was hoping to go to Whitman College in Walla Walla and was going to visit the campus while we were there. Part of me had a sneaking suspicion that there was a hidden agenda behind this Walla Walla trip—maybe to make it fun for Janie or for us to see where she might be in the future or something. It certainly wasn't going to be about *me*.

"You said if I asked, I could borrow clothes. And remember Acts 4:32."

"'All the believers were of one heart and mind, and they felt that what they owned was not their own; they shared everything they had,' " Janie quoted. Her ski trip was almost all financed *and* she'd memorized all of the verses so far. I only had that one. *I'd better get moving.*

She pulled something from the bottom of the pile and threw it at me. It was the beige sweater!

"No way," I said. "You're letting me borrow the beige sweater?"

"Quick, take it before I change my mind," she said.

I didn't need to be told twice. I snatched the sweater, gave her a kiss on the cheek, and ran to finish packing.

My mom came into the room. "Do you need anything?"

"Are we going to church on Sunday while we're in Walla Walla?"

"Yes," Mom said. "There's one Dad wants to visit."

I didn't know my dad knew of any churches in Walla Walla. Maybe it was related to the guys he was talking with this week. Cool! If they were Christians and bought out the company, maybe good owners would have it for once. I could hope. I knew my dad did.

I finished packing all my beauty supplies and toiletries and jewelry and shoes—that took up half the suitcase—and then threw in the rest of the clothes. My fall uniform was pretty much the same—jeans or cargo pants, and a sweater or a T-shirt under a hoodie.

Dad loaded everything into the car. I loved that we were driving together as a family. When I was little, before my dad worked so much, we used to take a lot of driving trips. We'd play Mad Libs in the car and my mom would have a dashboard deli—making sandwiches in the front seat and passing them back. In some ways we didn't have as much back then, and in some ways we had a lot more.

"I'm taking Brie next door," I said. I was glad I had only Brie and the fish now, since we were leaving for a few days. Lots of times I had an extra cat or two or a guinea pig or hamster or whatever. I made a little weekend case for the dog, put her in her crate, and headed next door.

"Hello, dear," Mrs. Kellie said when she answered the door. "Come on in."

I let the dog out of her crate and into the house.

Kitty was right there at Mrs. Kellie's heels. When Kitty saw Brie, she arched her back at first, but then Brie ran circles around her before sitting still. Kitty sniffed at her, dismissed her as a foreign being, and went to sit in the living room.

"Here's her food." I handed over two cans of dog food. "She's so small she doesn't eat much. We'll be back Sunday night."

"I'm glad to help, dear. You were such a help to care for Kitty for me, and I had so many other things to attend to when Frank died. I wouldn't know what to do without Kitty. She makes the silence bearable."

I sighed. I wanted to win that contest. All those elderly people wanted was someone to warm the nights and have a tinkling collar or kitty bell to break the quiet of the apartment. Someone real and live to lick their hands in love. It wasn't too much to ask. It really wasn't.

On the way home, I saw Justin loading the trunk. "Why the long face?" he asked.

"Oh, just thinking about the pets I signed up to give to the lonely elderly. Pets that might die other-wise."

I could see Justin about to make a wisecrack, and my eyes filled with tears.

"You really care about the people and the pets, don't you?" he said.

I nodded. "I just came back from Mrs. Kellie's."

He put his heavy arm on me. "You'll win," he said. "You'll win."

We drove off into the dusk, Justin missing a football game, Janie missing a party, Mom missing a meeting. Dad on his way to a meeting. Me just glad to be squished in between them again in the backseat for once. We left the twinkling lights of Lewiston and Idaho behind and drove across the bridge to Washington. I sent a silent prayer for Kate as I passed by. She'd probably be talking with Kyle right now.

"*Wait!*" I said. "I forgot to email a file to Kate."

"What?"

"She needs it, Dad. She needs it to work on her song. She's only got ten days to work on the song before the final tryouts."

"You can write a song in that time," Dad said, unwilling to turn the car around.

"I can, but she can't."

"We're already on our way. You can call her." I heard in his voice that it was final.

"Does *anybody* in this car care about what is important to me?" I asked. "If we'd forgotten your papers or Mom's makeup bag or Janie's purse, would we turn around? Kate's my first good friend in a long, long time and I don't want to let her down." My eyes welled with tears again. What was wrong with me?

I saw my mom look at my dad out of the corner of her eye. Dad said, in a softer voice, "We'll go back."

He turned the car around. No one said anything bad to me. Justin didn't elbow me and Janie didn't snort. They didn't say anything supportive, either. I guess that was the best I could hope for.

I ran into my room and quickly pulled up my music folder on my computer. I clicked on a song that I'd written and attached it to a message and sent it to Kate without even a note. The car was still idling in the driveway.

When I got back into the car, my mom passed around a bag of chocolate chip cookies. We never ate cookies that weren't low fat.

When we pulled into Walla Walla a few hours later, the town was sleepy. We drove into the parking lot of the Marcus Whitman hotel. I thought it was very cool to stay there. Marcus and Narcissa Whitman were martyrs who had come to share their Christian faith with the local American Indian tribes a long time ago. I thought about Kyle, Kate's friend, who was a Christian Nez Perce. I wonder if Marcus and Narcissa could look from heaven and see that some of their native friends now believed in Jesus— in fact, were leaders and missionaries themselves.

"A suite! Nice." Justin walked into the hotel room

and tossed his duffel bag on the pull-out couch. Mom and Dad got their own room, and Janie and I would sleep in the second bed. We put our jammies on and watched cable TV from the bed.

"Tomorrow we'll visit the college while Dad has his meetings," Mom said. "Are you excited?"

Janie smiled. Whitman College was her first choice. I felt weird when Mom said that. I kind of wished Janie wasn't going. She was a pill, but we had a lot of good times, too. She was kind of like the North Star of womanhood to me. How would I find my way when she left? She didn't say anything, but she scooted closer to me on the bed.

The next morning, my dad had already left by the time we got going. I knew he was leaving, of course, since we were in the suite together, but he'd let us sleep in.

"First stop, Whitman College," Janie said as she jumped out of bed. Well, Janie doesn't really jump. She kind of does that cool-girl slither out of bed. She ran into the bathroom and locked it before Justin could get in.

"First stop, *breakfast*," Justin grumbled. He put the pillow over his head. I put one over mine, too.

My mom was already up and dressed. She always got up when my dad got up.

We had the continental breakfast downstairs. My mom was encouraging us to eat fruit and oatmeal—

healthy stuff—so she must have felt pretty confident that my dad's meetings would go okay. Otherwise we'd be allowed to eat comforting Pop-Tarts.

"Will we find out how Dad's meetings go right away?" I asked.

"I think so," my mom said.

"So we might know tonight that Daddy is unemployed?" Janie asked. "Exactly how will we pay for college then?"

College! How were we going to pay for the house and food and gas and everything else? Leave it to Janie to look out for number one. Justin looked sick, too. I think he realized how serious things were.

"Let's be tourists for a day," my mom said. "I'd like to get to know the town. It'll be fun and distract us."

We left the plush lobby and drove out into the town.

Walla Walla is a nice place. It has a cool downtown and lots of restaurants and stuff. Maybe I'd want to go to college there, too. After all, Janie would have already graduated since she's four years ahead of me, so I wouldn't have to go through college as "Genius Janie's little sister." Would I? Or was that what my whole life held?

We walked around the campus for a while and had lunch. Justin wanted to see what the athletic fields looked like.

"Can we see the music rooms?" I asked.

"This isn't about you," Janie said. Justin mimicked her behind her back. I giggled.

"It might be someday," I said.

"Yes, you can," Mom said. I straightened up.

The music rooms were beautiful. The walls were padded, and there was an awesome grand piano in the middle of the recital hall.

The student who had been assigned to show us around sat down and played "Chopsticks."

Chopsticks. "May I play the piano?" I asked.

"Sure," he said.

Instead of playing "Chopsticks," though, I played the beginnings of "Follow Me." It wasn't going to be ready for me to play at the tryouts, I knew that. It was coming slowly. It was going to be the best song I ever wrote. If I won, and if I continued my life in music, it would be the first song I'd want to play in public, wherever that may be. If I lost, and my ministry in music was over before it even started, it would be my swan song.

"That is beautiful," the student guide said when I stopped halfway. "Can you finish it?"

"I can," I said. "But I haven't."

Even Janie looked at me with interest. For a minute anyway.

"Let's drive by the church we're going to tomorrow," Mom said. "I want to know where it is so we're not late."

"If things go badly with Dad today, are we still going to visit that church?" I asked.

"Of course." My mom looked puzzled. "Why wouldn't we?"

We began our drive back to the hotel. All of a sudden I saw a dog dash out into the road. It wore tags, but no person seemed to be in control of it. I saw a truck squeal around the corner. The dog looked confused. Which way should it go?

"Stop, Mom!" I shouted. She slammed on the brakes but the truck didn't. I saw it hit the dog. The truck never stopped; it just screamed away.

"Oh no," Justin said, snapping off his seat belt.

I barely waited till Mom came to a complete stop before I jumped out of the backseat. The dog was at the side of the road. They say that hurt animals often bite those who try to help them, and sometimes they do, but this one didn't. He looked at me with sad eyes and licked my hand. He didn't seem to have any internal injury, but his leg looked bent backward, and he whimpered when I tried to move him.

"Hold on, Buddy," I said, reading his name and his owner's number from his tag. I called out the phone number to my mom. "Call them and tell them we have their hurt dog." Janie stood silently by. "Can you find out what street we're on?" I asked. She ran down to the end of the street and looked at the sign.

We loaded the dog onto a board my dad kept in

the trunk for putting messy items on, like paint cans and stuff that he didn't want on the trunk floor.

"No one answered," my mom said, putting the phone away and starting up the car. "But I left a message."

The downtown was pretty small. We drove up and down a couple of streets till we found an animal shelter.

We carried Buddy into the shelter office. Janie stayed with the car. She didn't roll her eyes, but she didn't help in any way. Frankly, I was too busy to worry about it.

"Hello, this dog was just injured in a hit-and-run," I said. "I think his leg is broken, but otherwise he looks okay. No internal bleeding, I don't think."

The receptionist looked at me. "How do you know all of this?" she asked.

"I, ah, work with animals," I said more quietly. I hadn't realized how bold I'd been.

"We can take care of him here," she said. "Our staff vet is in today doing low-cost spaying and neutering, so we'll have her look at him." She peered at me over her glasses. "Where do you work with animals?"

"At home," I said. "I live in Lewiston."

"Well, thanks so much."

I gave Buddy a pat, knowing he'd be okay as soon as the vet took care of him. Then we left.

"You're a different person lately," Justin said.

"What do you mean?"

"I don't know. More take-charge."

Maybe I've always been that way, but you've never noticed, I thought. I didn't say it though. I didn't want to dis him after the compliment.

We made it back to the hotel in time for a good hour of cartoons before Dad got back.

No one spoke right away. My mom finally spoke up first in a too-bright voice. "So, how did it go?"

"I don't know," Dad said. "They haven't made a decision, but they will in the next few days. Either way, it doesn't look good for us, dear. If they don't buy the company, we'll close the doors. If they do buy the company, they'll bring in their own management to run it the way they do their current plant."

"Why wouldn't that be good?" I asked.

Janie shot daggers at me. "Because if they bring in their own management, they won't need the management that's there. Namely, Dad and the other managers."

Oh. So either way, my dad might be out of a job.

"Let's go to dinner," my dad said. "And really celebrate."

"Celebrate what?" Justin asked. We were all wondering the same thing.

"Being a family," Dad said. "Being able to be tested and see that God will take care of us. We haven't had to depend on Him in this way for a long while."

The restaurant was, well, awesome. There were four dinners to choose from, and each separate meal had five courses. I was worried, of course, that there wouldn't be a vegetarian choice.

Dad and Justin ordered the steak. And frog legs. Ick. Mom ordered the chicken.

"I'll take the vegetarian course," Janie said.

What?!

I didn't show my surprise in front of the waiter. "Me too," I said.

"I have to go to the bathroom," I said as soon as the waiter left.

"Thanks for the announcement," Justin said. I frowned at him.

"Do you want to come?" I asked Janie. She nodded.

When we were washing our hands, I said, "So, what's up with the vegetarian menu?"

"I didn't want you to be the only one," she said. "You always are. I thought it might be lonely."

I felt misty-eyed again. It was so cool. See? This whole thing with the contest *was* drawing my family's attention to me. Good was coming out of it. More good was going to come out of it, and I felt sure that taking care of Buddy was a sign that things were going to go right for the other animals.

I didn't want to lose and have Janie go back to eating steak and Justin go back to giving me a noogie. My mom might not stop at the music rooms like she did at the college today. Dad might not turn the car around for me anymore. Finally I was speaking their language. The language of success.

Please, God, let me win and be successful and be totally, fully the same as the rest of my family.

⌇

The next morning, we packed and checked out of the hotel before church so we could just head home after the service. Everyone's mind was busy. Dad and Mom were wondering what was going to happen with the company and with Dad's job. One of the men he'd met with the day before would be at church, I knew, and I wondered if Dad felt weird about meeting him again.

"Bob's going to be there," Dad said again once we were on our way. Aha. He *was* nervous. I was glad that my mom had scoped out the route the day before.

"Are you coming to the church service with us or going to the teen class?" Mom asked the three of us.

"Church," Janie and Justin said.

"Teen group," I said, even though I didn't really want to. I wanted them to keep respecting me and my bravery. That way, if I lost, maybe they'd remember these other things.

Dad took me to the communications center, introduced me, and asked the woman there where the junior high Sunday school met.

"I'll take her," a guy about my age behind the counter said.

The woman looked over. "Thanks, Jake." Then to my dad she said, "My son. He's in eighth grade."

Jake and I walked down the hall. I sure hoped he liked to make small talk, since I'm not too good at that—especially with cute guys I'd just met! I was kind of worried that it'd be a small room and everyone would stare when we walked in.

"So, where are you visiting from?" Jake asked.

"Lewiston, Idaho," I answered. "My dad is here on business, and my sister is checking out Whitman College."

"Good music program," he said. He ran his hand through his dark, curly hair.

I brightened. "Do you play an instrument?"

"Guitar," he said. "I just started giving lessons. It's a way to make some money to support my ski habit." He smiled and it warmed me. I smiled back.

"I play keyboard and write music," I said in a

rush. *Why am I talking so much?* "But I'd like to learn more about guitar," I babbled. "I just bought one."

"Very cool," he said. "I haven't written too much music." He opened the door. "We're here."

The room was as big as the one at my church at home, which was cool. I knew Kate liked her small church, but I liked a bigger one. The room went quiet, and then a few girls came over to me.

"Hi, are you Jake's friend?" one asked.

I was just about to explain that I was new and visiting, but Jake stepped in. "Yep. She's my friend Paige, from Lewiston, Idaho. And she writes music."

"Cool," one girl said. "You can sit over here." One girl, however, turned her back to me and went to talk with another group. I guess populars were in every church.

Even so, the hour flew by.

Afterward the kids downed doughnuts and hot chocolate. I ate one and talked with the girls and Jake and his buddies for a while.

I don't know why I did it. Maybe because I wanted them to like me or maybe because they were so nice I felt like I could be myself. But when they all started talking about what they were doing next week, I mentioned the final auditions.

"Cool," Jake said. "Don't worry," he said with confidence. "You'll win." He wrote his email address down on a slip of paper. "We're all in a small prayer group at youth group on Wednesday night," he said, motioning to the others nearby. "We'll pray for you this week. Email and let us know how it goes."

Too bad I'd never see him again.

I met up with my family, and even Dad seemed to be a little more relaxed, even though he was talking with a man I thought must be Bob.

On the way home, Justin put his headphones on, Mom and Dad talked business, and Janie napped. I doodled a shaggy dog—cute, friendly, loyal, and smart. The only thing was, the person I had in mind as a model really wasn't a dog at all. He was a curly-headed guitar player. I felt my face grow warm.

Yikes!

CHAPTER EIGHT
clarkston, washington

kate

Yikes!

I couldn't believe that Paige had sent me "Follow Me"—her best, new, unfinished song—to use as a model. I just couldn't believe it She hadn't even been willing to sing the whole thing to me—or any of it, really. She just told me that it was the most important song she'd ever written, and now that I looked it over I could see why. The way she set up the refrain to change but use the first and second word in the lines was genius. Why wasn't she using it herself?

I sat in my room after reading it. Paige was offering the very best of herself. She didn't hold back and offer me second best. She gave me the red bracelet to wear before she'd even worn it, even if Kyle hadn't appreciated the gesture! I sat down and started writing right away. The song was just what I had needed.

I pulled out my guitar and strummed a few chords. Not her chords, of course, my own, but in that pattern. Lots of songs had similar patterns. Right?

I practiced my song for a long time in my room and then decided it would be the one I would submit. I looked out my window at the bowing apple tree.

Lord, that was such a good gift. I feel bad that I thought all rich people were selfish and snobby and that I misjudged my friend so badly. What can I do to make a good gift in return?

I snapped my fingers. Pass the good on to someone else! Vickie. That's what I could do. I'd talk with her Monday at school. I'd just follow Paige's example.

Before I left my windowsill I spied the house on the other side of the twins'. Oh! I had completely forgotten that they wanted to talk with me. I told my mom where I was going, slipped my hands into some fuzzy mittens, and wrapped a scarf around my neck before walking over there.

I stopped by Nancy and Lee's mailbox and put an

envelope in there with a dollar for each of them, lunch money I had saved. I knew they loved the dollar store. It would be a fun trip for them.

I kept walking and then knocked on the neighbors' door. The mom answered. "Yes?"

"Hi," I said. "I'm Kate Kennedy. I baby-sit the twins. Their mom said you wanted to talk with me about something?"

"Come in," she said. I stepped into their neat house. "Have a seat."

I sat on the very edge of a slippery tan satin couch. It feels weird being in someone else's house when you don't know them very well. Not like I thought an ax murderer was going to jump out or something; I mean, my mom knew I was here. But still.

"We are moving," the mom said.

"Yes, I'd heard," I said. "I'm sorry."

"Oh, I am not," she said. "We finally got a job near family in California, so it will be a nice move. However, we have a kitten."

Okay, now I wondered. Weren't kittens allowed in California?

"We will have to live with my parents for a while when we move there, and their condo association doesn't allow pets. We didn't know that when we got her."

"Oh." I guess there wasn't going to be baby-sitting, but I still wasn't sure what she was asking me to do.

"Kate, I am wondering if you'd be willing to adopt her.

The twins' mom says they are too little for a young cat. If you take her, I'll give you a year's worth of food. She is spayed and all up to date on her shots. I do not want her to go to the pound."

Yeah, right. I couldn't take a cat. I didn't know anything about taking care of animals. My parents would say no because pets cost money.

Still, kittens were so cute. I hated to see her get sent to the pound or something. "I know someone who can solve your problem," I said. "I think. Can I call you later this week and let you know?"

"Sure, Kate," she said. She looked puzzled. I think she was expecting *me* to solve her problem. And I would, in a way. With Paige.

I went home and left a message on Paige's machine. "Call me right away!" I wanted to thank her for the song and to see if she wanted this kitten. I looked out my window again and saw the little thing tiptoeing in the yard two doors down, then batting a leaf on the wind. She was too cute to go to the pound. I'd noticed her before, of course, but now I had a special interest.

The next day, Monday, I started walking to school

early. I wanted to see if I could catch Vickie and talk with her about youth group. I had an idea she'd be excited about my plan, but I wasn't sure.

I finally caught up with her at lunch. "Vickie!" I said. She turned and looked at me with real delight. I realized I hadn't ever initiated a friendship with her in any way. I felt bad. Had I misjudged her, too? Was I ever going to do anything right?

"Hi, Kate," she said.

"Can we talk for a minute?"

"Sure." We sat down at a lunch table; it was still sticky with ketchup. I tried to set my bag on a clean square on the floor. Must be a guy table first lunch period.

"Are you watching the kids again at church this Wednesday night?" I bit into an apple. One of the ol' pucker-faced ones.

Vickie's face fell a little. "Yes. Carrie doesn't have anyone else."

"I don't mind watching them," I said. "And I think you should lead youth worship."

Vickie had been going to eat a fry but she dropped it. "You do? I mean, I've done it for you when you've been sick or gone, but you want me to take your place?"

Now, that was a little too much. "No, I don't want you to take *my* place. I think we should each have our own place in worship."

"Thanks," she said, beaming. When we were done eating, she walked off with her other friends and I went to return a book to the library. While I was there I checked out a book on cats. I don't know why, really.

Paige had emailed that she'd come down with a cold on the way home from Walla Walla but had a story to tell me about a dog named Buddy that got hurt and someone named Jake who was *not* a dog. Ha-ha. I had no idea what that meant. She said she'd call when she felt better. I really, really missed talking with her. I hadn't realized how much I valued her friendship.

Wednesday night at church I sat in the middle of the floor and played patty-cake and made play dough cakes and pretended to eat them over and over again. I looked at the cross hanging above the door. Wasn't this what I said I wanted to do on the reservation?

That gave me an idea.

"Let's learn 'Jesus Loves Me,'" I said. I took my guitar out of the case, and then I sang the song and taught it word by word to the kids. When I sat down in the middle of the floor and played my guitar, each of them quieted down and listened. When I finished, they clapped. They sang it with me. Many of them knew it, but sang it like they were singing it for the first time, with excitement and hand clapping and joy in their eyes.

"Jesus loves me," one little guy said in wonderment. "Jesus loves me." He said it to anyone who came to the door. My eyes filled with tears. No spotlight, only the quiet blue-and-white lamp from the nursery. No crowd. Well, a crowd of toddlers. The sweetest voices ever. One little girl looked like Katie used to. She kissed my cheek after dropping her juice box.

God, please help me get the money to help those kids on the reservation somehow, too. They deserved to have gifts like every other kid. But my winning meant Paige's losing. Could I figure out a way for us both to win? I thought about it all the way home and prayed. By the time I got, there I figured I had the solution. I wanted to win. I wanted Paige to win. Could we both?

I went straight to the computer and quickly typed a note to the Worship Works people.

> *Hello, I was wondering if there is a way for two people to win the Turkey Bowl contest. I know you had us sing "The Star-Spangled Banner." Could one person perform at half time and one sing the opening? Can two people sing a duet? Please respond right away.*

There wasn't any guarantee that the two of us would come in at numbers one and two of the five finalists, of course, but with our helping each other it seemed a real possibility. What if they did let us? Would we split the money? It still wouldn't be enough for us both to get what we need. But maybe it would be something. I hoped he'd email back right away. Paige had left a message. I'd wait till tomorrow to call her back, because maybe I'd have good news. In fact, it seemed like a perfect solution! I thought it would surely come to pass. Surely God would want us to share, right? Just like Paige shared her clothes and I was sharing the singing with Vickie? Maybe that's what this was all about!

I sat down at the computer. "Dear Paige," I wrote. "I hope you're feeling better. Can't wait to talk with you. I have lots of good news to share."

I knew that when she called I *would* have good news to share.

That night my dad came home late from working the night shift at Rainmaker. He had the car since we'd gotten a ride to church so my mom wouldn't have to drive out late and get him. I was in bed, but I heard them. My parents hardly ever argue, so when they do it's a big deal. I tried not to listen. No, that's not true. I listened. Our walls are as thin as T-shirts.

"There is nothing I can do," Dad said. "If the company is bought, I will have a job, and if they aren't, I won't."

"Then you should start looking for a new job right now. We don't have a week's worth of pay to cover things!" Mom said. "I would know, because I pay the bills."

Ouch. That was a sting.

"I'm sorry," she said right afterward. "But we have to do something."

"We can trust in the Lord to provide," my dad said. Even his voice sounded uncertain.

I could hear the tension in Mom's voice. "Just when

will we know what's going to happen?"

"In a few days," Dad said. "I'm sure of it."

"Yes, you'll find out you're laid off at the same time as everyone else, except on second shift and not first, and then the jobs will already be gone." My mom stalked out of the kitchen and into the bedroom, closing the door just controlled enough not to qualify as a slam.

I felt sick. My ears literally burned, because I didn't want to hear any of this. My heart burned, too. Not with indigestion. With sorrow. I stuffed a pillow over my head. I could still hear the voices. I put my headphones and music on and the voices faded away.

"Remember us," I said to God, not trusting myself to say anything else right now because it might be disrespectful. "Please remember us."

I listened to one CD, then took my headphones off. The house was quiet. I fell asleep to the howling November wind; it cried in the darkness as it twisted off of the river. I hoped that kitten was inside. I hoped everything would be okay, but how could it be? Even if I won, I'd have to spend the winnings helping my family make it till my dad got a new job. A tear slid down my face and onto my pillow. I let it go without wiping it away.

The next morning I checked the computer right away. No message from Worship Works. Paige had written back, though.

"Still on for our Thursday get-together tonight to practice our songs?" she asked. "I'm feeling better, going to school today, and looking forward to filling you in on all my juicy news. Not that anything will come of it. Call me right after school or else I'll just count on your being at my house. Paige."

School dragged by, of course. Work, work, work. Friends, of course. No music. I hoped Paige would be psyched when she saw what I'd done with my song, with her idea.

I got home just before my mom would take me to Paige's. I quickly checked my email and found a response from Worship Works! Yahoo! I knew they'd come through in enough time, and now I would have something great to share with Paige, too.

Dear Miss Kennedy,

Thank you for your concern about all of the contestants. There are certainly many places to share the stage, but this contest is not one of them. Clarkston High School has already selected someone to sing "The Star Spangled Banner"; we simply chose that song because most contestants had some familiarity with it. Our contest is for a single singer-songwriter.

*There will be many other contests, some of them
duets or bands, I'm sure. But not this one. We're
looking forward to your final audition on Monday.*

Sincerely,
Worship Works Staff

My fingers stumbled over the right keys to close down
the message, the Internet, the computer. I had heartburn
again. I had tried. Maybe neither of us would win, and
then, while there would be lots of problems for both of
us, at least there would be no problem between us as
friends.

Now what was I going to tell Paige about my good
news? And how would our friendship look a week from
now when the contest was complete?

"Ready to go?" Mom grabbed her purse and Dad his
dinner and we headed toward the door. Mom would
drive me over, of course, after dropping Dad off at work.
Mrs. Winsome would take me home. Or Janie. Secretly, I
hoped it was Janie. Paige had no idea how cool it was to
have an older sister to drive you places, playing good
music and making snappy conversation. Plus, she
chewed gum. Gum chewers are right on. I tugged on my
GummyWears necklace.

We got there soon enough. "Hi, Kate," Mrs. Winsome
said. It was funny. I knew things were looking down for
them at work, but she looked more relaxed than she had

in a while. She let me into her beautiful home. It smelled good, like she was actually cooking!

"What's up with your mom?" I asked Paige as we ran to her room.

"What do you mean?"

"She looks, well, mellow."

Paige smiled. "She quit teaching Bible study."

I wrinkled my brow. "That would make her mellow?"

"It would if she weren't doing twenty thousand things anymore."

Aha. I was glad for my friend. "First, the important part. Tell me about your trip and the mysterious dogs." As I said the word *dogs*, Brie climbed up on my lap.

"Well, we had a great time, and on Saturday morning we saw a dog get hit by a car. We ran him to a shelter nearby."

"Cool," I said. I saw her face fall. "I mean, not cool that the dog was hit. Cool that you could help."

She nodded. "It was cool," she said. "And it reminded me how much I love caring for animals. I had asked God for a sign that I was going to win the contest and provide for those two I signed up for. I thought maybe this would be it. . . ."

She looked at me and her voice trailed off. Honestly, neither of us quite knew what to do with the fact that we both still wanted to win, and yet neither of us wanted the other to lose.

"Tell me about the dog behind Door Number Two," I said.

"He"—Paige smiled—"was definitely not a dog. His name's Jake. He plays guitar, he was nice, he called me his friend. He and his prayer group are going to pray for me—hey, they must have prayed last night, Wednesday. He gave me his email address." She held up a doodled-on piece of paper. I snatched it from her.

"Hey!"

There was the email addy, a cute sheepdog/nice-looking boy doodle, and a heart. "Is this a heart?" I asked.

"No, it's a flower," she answered.

"A heart-shaped flower," I said. I giggled with her. "I know what movie my mom and I will watch tonight."

"What?"

"*Ever After*. For you."

She threw a pillow at me, and we ran downstairs to her music room, where we started to get set up. I unzipped my guitar case.

"What good news did you have?" she asked. "I'm sorry I hogged up the whole time up there."

I swallowed my gum. I wished for something good to tell her about Worship Works.

I thought fast. "It's about a new pet for you."

"What?" Paige stopped opening up her piano and sat down on the bench.

"It's a kitten. The cutest little kitten." I explained about the neighbors moving and how they'd give a full year's supply of food.

"Mmm-hmm," Paige said, stretching her fingers. "What makes you think I want a kitten?"

"This cat is headed toward the pound. Do you *ever* turn down an animal in need?"

"Yes," she said, sitting on the bench.

I couldn't believe it. Paige was going to let a kitten go?

"You're just going to let it go to the *pound*?"

"No. *You* are going to take it. Unless your mom would object. But there's really no expense involved. And cats, especially indoor-outdoor cats, are low maintenance."

I sat down. "No, you don't understand. I don't know what to do with a cat."

"I'll teach you. I'll give you a good list of ideas, and I'll be here anytime to talk about it with you. Just like you did for me baby-sitting Valerie!"

She opened her sheet music and turned on the mic. "I think maybe you guys should watch *Aristocats* tonight."

She got me. I giggled. My own pet. I guess it could be true.

I walked over and gave her a quick hug. "Thank you. That's the second great gift you've given me this week, although it doesn't match up to the first." I took a swig of my Coke.

Paige turned around. "What do you mean?"

"You know, the song. 'Follow Me.' When you said you were going to send a song for me to copy the style from,

I had no idea you'd upload your best, precious new one to me. It inspired me to do lots of great things this week. And I've been working really, really hard on a new song, based on that one. In fact, I had a great idea. . . ." I noticed Paige was kind of pale. It was chilly down here.

"Are you okay?" I asked. She nodded but seemed kind of dazed.

I thought she was going to faint. I ran over toward her. "Paige, are you all right?"

CHAPTER NINE
lewiston, idaho

paige

"Paige, are you all right?"

"What?"

"I said," my sister Janie repeated, "are you all
right? You look bomb-shocked or something."
We'd just left Kate's house after having dropped
her off. I *felt* bomb-shocked ever since she'd
brought that up. My song. My *new* song!

"I'm fine." I pulled my jacket more tightly

around my body and turned the music in the car up so Janie wouldn't ask me any more questions. I'd been able to fake it pretty well, I think, till we took Kate home after rehearsing together in my downstairs. I didn't want Kate to know the truth. The truth was, this had totally rocked my world.

The time between Clarkston and Lewiston clicked by. The river kept flowing. The wind kept blowing. We drove over the bridge and home again, so simple. Why couldn't life be simple?

I'd sent Kate "Follow Me." I hadn't meant to. Now what was I going to do?

I don't know what the worst of it was, the fact that I'd accidentally sent her the best thing I'd ever written and had her pick it apart and use it for her own, or the fact that she thought I had offered her my very best when I hadn't. I hadn't meant to give her such an expensive present, and now I was getting credit for something I didn't do. I knew if I told her it was a mistake, though, she'd immediately stop writing the song she'd been working so hard on. The song she was planning to sing in four days. I knew she couldn't write songs very fast. She'd have to start over.

I turned toward the car window, my breath close enough to make fog circles. When I was a little girl I used to draw hearts or my initials or doodle dogs in the center of those circles. This time I drew question mark after question mark in the circles, which disappeared without offering answers.

What should I do? If I told her it was a mistake, she'd give it back, my unfinished song would really be mine again, and I'd be able to keep it close and hidden like my other notebooks. Until it was done. But then she'd have nothing to sing at the contest, and she'd know the truth about me, that I really wasn't ready to sacrifice anything major for her.

Maybe I am ready to do that. The thought came from me, and to me, but it seemed more like it was from God. I don't know.

"Moody," Janie muttered under her breath as we pulled into the driveway.

I went into my room, planning to write Paige an email telling her how sorry I was that I had sent her the wrong song and that it was a big mix-up but that I needed it back and hoped she wouldn't use it. But our ISP was down. I'd do it later tonight.

"Too late to go for a walk?" My mom came up behind me.

"No," I said. Was I in trouble, or was this just a part of the new-and-improved Mom?

"Anyone else coming?" I asked.

"No, just you and me."

I put on my boots and a heavier jacket and we clomped down the road a bit.

Once you got out of our driveway, there were

other houses on the lane. Far apart, it was true. You could see the lights twinkling through their frosted panes. I loved living in my neighborhood. Every summer we'd have a huge block barbecue where we drew names to see who brought what dish. We showed up with zany things, like potato salad with pickles in it or hamburgers shaped like Mickey Mouse.

During the winter, neighbors competed to see who could decorate their houses the fanciest. Before my dad got really busy, he used to dress up as Santa Claus right before Christmas and stand outside with me. Just me. Because I sang carols. All the neighbors came, and Mr. Kellie used to sing along with me.

"So how was your day?" my mom asked. Did she really want to know, or was she just worried that her concept of a good mom would be ruined if she didn't?

"Good," I said. "Well, kind of hard." I decided to be brave and tell her about the song. If she just dismissed it or said, "It will all work out okay," I would never, ever tell her anything private again.

"I sent the wrong song to Kate," I said as I stuffed my hands into my pockets. "I sent her the new one I was working on."

"I didn't know you were working on a new song," Mom said.

"Yeah, it's called 'Follow Me,'" I said. "I came up

with a new technique with the lyrics, using two words from the first lines in the refrain. Anyway, when I sent a file to Kate before we went to Walla Walla last week, I sent the wrong song."

"I'm sorry," Mom said. "Can you ask for it back?"

I nodded. "Yes. But she'll be very disappointed and she won't have anything good for the contest."

My mom hugged me. "It sounds tough."

That was it. No lecture or problem solving. No wandering mind. No pretending that it didn't hurt. Maybe when she wasn't so busy the real mom came out. I slipped my hand through hers and we walked back home.

When I was a little girl, I used to pretend to smoke in the cold air, blowing it out through my mouth. My mom would always scold me and follow it up with a lecture about the evils of smoking. I knew that. I was just having fun.

I blew smoke out of my mouth just to see what would happen. My mom wagged her finger. Some things never changed. But when I turned to look back, she was blowing smoke, too. I giggled.

We got home, and I wrapped my scarf around the peg in the front hall and kicked my boots under the bench. I walked into the living room, where my dad was sitting head-to-head with Janie.

Janie looked like she'd been crying. Wow. She hadn't seemed sad when we took Kate home. Maybe she'd had a fight with her boyfriend of the month.

"Everything okay?" I asked. My dad nodded and put his arm around me.

"We're all going to Justin's game tomorrow, okay?" Dad said. Justin was still at practice—he started in the game tomorrow.

"Sure." It'd be fun. Walter would be there, and so would Hayley, that new girl from our church whom I'd met at the pool with Kate. It was nice to have a friend in youth group for a change. Maybe we could all start a prayer group like that church in Walla Walla had. Just us. Not Mallory.

When I went to bed that night, I still hadn't e-mailed Kate. It just felt like static electricity was zapping unseen around my house.

On Friday I figured it was do or die. There were only three days till the final tryouts, only two weeks till Thanksgiving. I needed to call Kate at this point if I was going to call at all.

I got home, went into my room, and sat on my bed with my dog. My mom had set a huge stack of clothes on my bed and I started to put them away.

Kate had returned the red sweater she'd worn at her dinner with Kyle, too.

The red sweater. I hadn't felt so good letting her wear it after me. But why? After all, the sweater was mine. I wouldn't mind letting her borrow, say, my jean jacket, and I'd worn that many times.

I sat on my bed and doodled in a notebook. It always helped me to think. I realized the red sweater bugged me because I had worried that if Kate wore it to the first tryouts, she'd look and sound better than I would. It was my wanting to be better, and who could blame me? I wanted to win, too.

I sighed. I couldn't do it. It had been my mistake to send the song. She shouldn't have to pay. I knew it was the right thing to do, but I was still mad.

If she wins, I told God, *it'll be because of me.* I picked at a thread in my bedspread.

If she wins, I heard in my heart, *it will be because of* Me.

I sat there quietly, balling the red sweater up in my hand. I sighed. I knew that no matter who won, God allowed it. I just didn't know if I could live with that fact. With God. With Kate.

I didn't call her to say she couldn't have my song. I didn't call her to wish her a good weekend, either.

That night was one of the best Friday night football games we'd ever gone to. There were only two more weeks till the Turkey Bowl, and Justin's team was on fire. Justin played almost every quarter, and it was so fun to watch. I wore my hair tied back in a tie but still slipped my chopstick through it.

"That's cool." Hayley poked my chopstick.

"Thanks."

"Did I see your friend at the pool wearing one, too?" she asked.

"Yes," I said. Looking out at the team jerseys, I remembered why we'd decided to wear them. "Musicians don't have T-shirts or whatever, so it's kind of like our team symbol."

Hayley nodded.

Warmth spread through me. Kate and I were a team. One for all. All for one.

Hayley shared her hot chocolate with me, and we cheered the team. It would be cool to be in high school and actually cheer our friends. Next year boys our own age would be out there, playing in JV football.

Justin's team won, of course. We waited around while he showered up because we always went for pizza afterward as a family before Justin and Janie went on to parties.

Justin and some of his friends walked over. "Can they come to pizza?" he asked Dad. "They have their own money," he added quickly.

"Of course," Dad said.

Justin and Janie rode in their car, and I rode with Mom and Dad.

"Justin told us that you're going to sing at half time at the Turkey Bowl," one of his friends said after we'd been seated.

"Very cool," another buddy said. "I didn't know old croaky-voiced Justin here had a talented sister. Must have skipped over the middle child."

Justin blew a straw wrapper at him. "Hey, dude, you can drive yourself tonight if you want."

"No car," his friend answered.

"Exactly."

Even Janie smiled. Usually, talking to junior boys was beneath her. I know she was counting the minutes till she could be with her friends.

"Well, you cheer us during the game and we'll cheer for you when you sing at half time," Justin's other friend said to me.

"Hear, hear," they all said and clinked their Coke glasses together.

I smiled weakly. I knew no one else would say, "Hey, she might not win," because that would be so rude. On the other hand, did Justin tell them I was in it for sure?

"I still have to try out on Monday," I spoke up. But by then the conversation had turned. Justin winked at me. It was good to have my big brother be proud of *me* for once. Usually he was all suited up with all eyes on him.

Justin and his friends took Justin and Janie's car, and Janie came home with us to change and wait for her friends to pick her up. I sat on her bed, cross-legged.

"Where you going tonight?" I asked.

"Oh, a couple of parties," she said. She lined her eyes with eye shadow. "Want to try?"

I smiled and she shut her door. My mom didn't allow us to wear makeup before we turned sixteen, but I was just in the house, after all.

I put on some purple.

"You look bruised," Janie said. "I don't think that's the look you're after."

Brownish red. "Flame face."

Black eyeliner. "Clown." She tossed me a moss green. "Try this."

I smoothed a little on my lid, and she came back and ran a Q-tip over it and took half of it off. When I looked in the mirror, I loved how I looked.

"Oh, this is the best color for me," I said. "Can I have it?"

Janie tapped her foot. "Okay."

"Can I have your beige sweater?"

"Maybe when I go to college. If I get into Whitman."

I'd start praying for that right now.

"Can I have your bed when you go to college?"

"*No way!* Greedy." She threw a hair scrunchie at me.

I knew when I'd better get moving. I grabbed my new eye shadow and headed out of the room.

My mom caught me in the hall. "*What* is that?" she said.

"Eye shadow, from Janie. Come on, Mom, it looks good. I can wear it on Monday."

"Monday in two years, you mean?" My mom held out her hand.

"No, this Monday. In three days." I knew I'd feel really confident if I had it on. It would look so great with my army green cargo pants, too.

My mom kept her hand out. "Hand it over and I'll hand you some mail."

Reluctantly, I handed her the eye shadow pack. "I'll give it back in two years," she said. Then she handed over an envelope to me. It was from the shelter!

I took it into my room and opened it.

"Dear Miss Winsome," it began. Someone had scribbled "Paige!" in the margin. It must have been Margie, the shelter director.

Thank you for your generous offer to place two pets. You'll be glad to know that we have already selected and notified the two elderly recipients. One is a man who lost his wife this year and is so excited to be getting an adult dog—one he doesn't have to train. The dog needs a home, too, as its owners abandoned it. We'll be taking care of all of its medical bills, and it will be placed in early December.

My stomach felt sick.

We're also placing a cat with a woman whose cat was hit by a car last month. She had her daughter call us up and express her thanks as soon as she got the letter notifying her that the food will be provided, too.

I was breathing heavily now.

What can we say but thanks! *Please remit your funds by December 15, and feel free to call if you have any questions.*

At the bottom of the letter, Margie had scrawled, "Lots of fun stuff to do around here; hope to see you soon!"

I set the letter down on my computer. Then I folded it up, pulled back the towel covering the song-writing notebooks in my closet, and slipped the letter inside the top cover. I closed the closet doors.

The weekend seemed to fly by. I didn't practice on Sunday. It was the Sabbath.

Monday morning came. I got up really early, even though the audition wasn't till after school.

I called Kate. "Hi," I said. We'd never talked before school before. "Are you ready for tryouts?"

"I am," she said. "Are you?"

"Yep. My mom is going to take me. I'll meet you there."

"Have a good day," Kate said softly.

"You too," I said. I hung up, twisted my hair into a ponytail, and then slipped my chopstick through it. It was getting a little ragged and tore a piece of my hair when I stuck it in. It would be cool to get one of those pretty lacquered ones someday.

The day wore on. At free period I went into the music room and asked my choir teacher if I could practice in there.

"Of course," she said. "I'll be praying for you."

She'd heard about my tryouts. I didn't know she was a Christian.

I looked over the notes for my song. It was one I had started a little bit before "Follow Me." I did like it. It would probably be my second favorite song, even though I hadn't figured out my new technique when I wrote it. I could have done "Follow Me." It just didn't feel ready to me yet.

Janie picked me up after school and drove me

home. "Nervous?" she asked.

I nodded. She handed me a piece of Doublemint. "This always helps when I'm nervous," she said. I didn't know Janie got nervous about anything.

I changed the subject to take my mind off of things. "Have you noticed that Dad seems different lately?" I asked.

She nodded and looked at me out of the corner of her eye.

"He's softer or something," I said. "I think I like him better this way. When he doesn't seem to know everything. It's like when he's weaker he's more likeable."

"'My strength is made perfect in weakness,'" Janie quoted. I was impressed. That wasn't even one of the ski trip verses.

The car rattled along, and when we pulled into the driveway, my palms were wet.

I ran upstairs and changed clothes, then sprayed on some perfume, wishing for the moss green eyeshadow. Oh well.

I'd prepared a special envelope for Kate—a surprise. Should I mail it or just give it to her? This afternoon was already going to be kind of strange. I didn't want to distract her. I ran it to the mailbox and put up the flag. Our mail carrier wouldn't come till almost five.

I got into the passenger side of Mom's car. My

mom got in her side and sat down with me.

"Do you want me to pray?" she asked.

I nodded.

"Lord, we ask that you would help Paige to be calm, to help her voice be on key and strong, and, Lord, we ask that you would help her to win."

Mom started the car and handed me a plastic bowl with a lid on it.

"What's this?" I asked.

"It's your after-school snack," she said.

I popped open the lid. Inside was a bowl of cherries and grapes from a can of fruit cocktail.

"No pears," I said.

"No pears," Mom agreed. She smiled and held my hand. My eyes filled with tears.

When we pulled up at the Lewiston high school, Kate and her mom were already waiting.

"Would you guys wait out here?" Kate asked.

I agreed. I just admired her being so bold as to ask not only her mom but my mom, too. She did it respectfully, though.

They called Kate in first, of course. *Kennedy*. She hadn't shown me her completed song before she went in, and I was kind of glad she didn't. I didn't want to be freaked out the whole time by thinking of hers or mine or whose was better.

I sat in the hallway and prayed for her, though. Then I doodled on my notebook.

A shepherd. Two sheep.

She came out flushed. I knew her well enough by now to know how well she'd done. She'd totally scored. We didn't speak. I was last, of course. *Winsome.*

"Come in, Miss Winsome." The lady who had worn a business suit and a tie last time now had on a softer sweater set. It made me feel better. I don't know why. Maybe because it made *her* seem softer, too.

"Here's my song," I said. "I'm going to sing the one I wrote first, if that's all right."

"Go ahead," the man replied. "Will you accompany yourself on the piano?"

"Yes."

My hands and voice shook for the first few seconds, but then I forgot the others were in the room and my hands took over and did what they did naturally without my even thinking. They flew over the keys when the music was fast and caressed the keys when it was slow. The room swallowed the music, and the music became the air in the room. I hit the notes clearly, since Kate had showed me how to open my nasal passages. I finished well. I knew I had controlled the pacing, the emotion, and everything else.

"Well done, Miss Winsome," the lady in the soft sweater set said. "Well done."

I had done it! I knew I had done my best. I

remember reading one time that Jesus told one of His servants, "Well done." *Was that okay, Lord?* I felt that warmth envelop me again.

I still didn't know if I was going to win. I still didn't know if *God* had told me I was going to win. I had to admit that now. But I did know that He had told me to try.

I walked out into the hallway.

"Okay?" Kate asked.

"Okay," I said.

"We going to be okay?" Kate asked. I knew she meant as friends.

"We're going to be okay," I said. I meant it then. I didn't know for sure if I'd still mean it if she won and my pets went without homes and my people without something to love them. I wanted to believe it didn't matter.

We linked arms like younger girls—who cared?—and walked outside.

"We have a surprise," Mom said. "The four of us are going for Chinese!"

Yum. Steamy egg drop soup on a cold night. What could be better?

Since we were in Lewiston this time, we drove to Two Trees, Kate's car behind ours. Whenever we got to a stoplight, her mom blinked the lights at our car and my mom honked back. We laughed. I couldn't believe my mom would do that.

"You don't think I honk at strangers when I'm with Dad?" she asked.

"No!" I said. "As if."

Mom winked. "Well, you don't know everything."

We pulled into the parking lot, and Mom got quiet all of a sudden before we got out of the car. "When will you find out who wins?"

"Tomorrow," I said, hands folded in my lap. "They promised they wouldn't make us wait. The Turkey Bowl is less than two weeks away."

CHAPTER TEN
clarkston, washington

kate

"They promised they wouldn't make us wait. The Turkey Bowl is less than two weeks away."

"Well, then they should call this afternoon. Or this evening. But I have plans for us right now," Mom said. "We can't just hang out by the phone."

It was one of the few times when I really wished we had a cell phone. If we had a cell phone, we could just go where we wanted and not worry about missing a call. But my mom seemed so cheery, and I didn't want to let her down.

"Okay," I said. "Where are we going?"

"Shopping."

Shopping? With what money? For what? Groceries? I didn't want to ask. I didn't want to know. I just wanted to go!

Mom took my hand and led me to the mailbox. "First we're going to check the mail."

"Okay, but don't we have to get Dad to work soon?" My dad never took off Tuesday, for goodness' sake. Maybe a Friday once in a while. "Is Dad sick?"

Mom shook her head. "Get the mail."

So I did. "There are two things for me here!" I said. One was a card from Kyle and Katie. One was a little padded envelope from Paige.

I opened Kyle's first. "Just a card to wish you well," the outside read. "And let you know you're in our thoughts and prayers." Okay, so it was a pre-printed standard card. But there was a bouquet of flowers on the front. And he'd underlined the word "thoughts" twice! Or was that Katie? Nah, she was too young to underline that neatly. Hmm, did they know that putting the stamp upside down meant I Love You, or was that just a coincidence?

Inside was written, *"You're gonna be great. Email and let me know how it goes. Kyle."*

"Two Four Six Eight, Who Do We Appreciate? Kate! Love, Katie." Someone else's handwriting had written

that sentence, but Katie had signed her own large, un-evenly scrawled name. I drew the card close.

"Open the second package," my mom urged. "I'm surprised to see it. I was expecting the card from Kyle and Katie because their mom told me it was coming. What's in the one from Paige?"

I shrugged. Paige hadn't said anything to me at all. I looked at the postmark. Mailed yesterday.

I opened it, and out fell a tiny blue bell on a silver coil. A kitty bell. A really beautiful kitty bell.

My mom laughed.

"What's so funny?"

"Wait till you see where we're going." She started the car and I got in, backpack and all. I hadn't even been in the house.

I stuck a piece of gum into my mouth as we drove just a couple of miles down the road. It was mid-November, and the air was snappy. All the leaves were pretty much gone, apples and pears, too. Most of the gardens had been clipped back to sleep for the winter. The road was warm now, but by tonight it would be glossy with frost. A few minutes later we pulled into the pet store.

"You mean I get to keep the kitten for sure? What about the expense?" When I had brought it up with Mom as soon as the neighbors had asked me, she'd hesitated over the money.

Mom held out some bills. "They gave us some money to buy her a few things and to get food for the year. You can pick out a little pet bed and a cat tower for her to scratch on. She's not scratching my furniture!"

"No way," I said. "I promise."

We wandered through the aisles. My own pet! I never thought this would happen. I was going to have my own cat. I'd still let her outside, of course, so she could roam, but she was not going to have to sleep outside. I'd put her bed in my room. She could sleep in there if she wanted.

I pulled all the price tags off of everything right when we got in the car. We'd be ready as soon as we pulled into the driveway.

When we got home, I ran over to the neighbors to get her. "Thank you so much," the mom said. "It makes a world of difference to us."

I beamed. "To me, too."

I brought the kitten home—her name was Muffin—and let her roam around and find her way. Her fur was soft as cotton. I know everyone says that about their pet, but this time it was really truly true. Her eyes were blue and matched the bell Paige had sent.

When I walked in the door, my dad handed me a slip of paper with a number on it. "Someone called for you. From Worship Works."

I ran into the kitchen and grabbed the phone. I took twelve deep breaths. I sat down while it rang. Then I stood up. I twirled the phone cord around my pointer finger.

"Hello," I said. "May I speak with—" I looked at the name on the paper—"Carol?"

"This is Carol."

"This is Kate Kennedy, returning your call."

"Hello, Kate," she said. "I am calling with good news."

Good news!

"You've won our contest."

I won! My hands shook.

"All five of you are so very talented, but you stood out just a little bit above the rest. You have a wonderful, wonderful voice. But what really pushed you over the edge was your lovely song. We'd never heard an arrangement quite like that from someone as young as you."

"Thank you," I said. I knew if I tried to say anything else, I would choke or cry, my throat was so tight.

"The unique rhythm between the verses and refrain. Is that new for you?"

"Yes," I said. "My friend was showing me how just last week. She sent me her song to learn from."

"Oh." Carol went quiet. "It was your song entirely, though, correct? You didn't have help?"

I sat there. Now, what does *help* mean? Of course I had help. I mean, people looked at one another's work all the time. To make it better. To offer comments.

"What do you mean by help? I wrote the song. The notes and the words."

"Okay. As long as it is all your work in concept, design, music, and lyrics."

"Would having my friend show me the format count?" I asked. My hand shook. My heart quaked. I had to sit down before my knees buckled. I felt like I had that day in kindergarten when I had to do the Pledge of Allegiance in front of the whole school.

"Well," Carol answered, "I'm afraid that's something only you can decide. There's a fine line between help and collaboration. You'll need to determine that on your own."

I could barely speak. "May I have a day to pray about it?"

"You may," Carol said. "But I'll need to call the others no later than tomorrow afternoon. We'll have to get the announcement in the paper by Thursday."

I hung up the phone and sat in the kitchen alone. What was I going to do? What was the *right* thing to do? For me? For Paige? For Kyle and Katie and the kids? I felt nauseated. The heartburn was back. In fact, my whole body hurt.

I sighed and laid my head on the table. My mom came in and put her arm around one side, and my dad came in and put his arm around the other.

"I'm sorry you lost," Dad said.

"I won," I said. They each pulled back.

"What?"

"I won," I said. "But there's more to it than that. It's a long story."

"Sounds like it's an out-to-dinner night," Dad offered.

I looked up. Why *was* he home? Why were we going out to dinner? I brushed my hair, put it up in a chopstick, and we left.

I had the feeling that I had just dumped water on their firecrackers. The car was quiet. I tried to rejoice. I knew I'd have peace eventually. I felt it. I just didn't know what choice would lead to that peace. There was no easy answer.

We pulled into the Crab Cooker and took a table. After ordering a Coke and some homemade fries, my dad prayed for the meal and then started talking.

"I have some wonderful news," he said. "I'm keeping my job!"

I cheered. What a roller-coaster day! "That is *great* news!" If I'd been sitting next to them I'd have kissed them both. "What happened?"

"You can't say anything to anyone yet. The only reason I know is that Mark Winsome called me aside."

"Paige's dad?"

My dad nodded. "There won't be an official announcement till the day after Thanksgiving, but since he now knows us and understands that I work to support my ministry, he wanted to let me know."

"Do you think he knew you'd be looking for another job?" Mom asked.

Dad nodded. "Probably. And he knows this is the hardest time of the year for a pastor, in many ways. I think he didn't want me to be divided in my efforts."

"That is *so* nice," I said. "The whole family is great. Did I tell you that their mom is cooking now?"

My parents looked at me as if I had just landed from Pluto. I wasn't going to get into it. "Anyway, I'm going to tell Paige thank-you from me, too."

"NO!" My dad said it so loudly that the tables around us quieted down. He got all red and lowered his voice.

"What I mean is, you can't say anything yet. Not only because it's not public information yet, but because, well, Paige's dad is losing his job."

My jaw dropped and my eyes opened wide. "What?"

"The company that's buying us out already has a similar operation in Walla Walla. They're going to bring in their own management to run the place just like that plant," Dad said. "It's probably a good idea. None of the supervisors are too helpful, except for Mark Winsome. He doesn't want Paige to know till after Thanksgiving."

I held my breath. "Since he's so good, he'll probably find another job soon, right?"

The waitress brought our fries and refilled our pop. "Your dinners are being plated," she said. Mom nodded at her.

"I hope so, but I don't think he'll find another job too easily," Dad said. "There's not much manufacturing around here. I'm not sure what he can do," Dad said. "There will be no extra money. We have to remain extremely lean in order to keep Rainmaker running. No raises. No overtime. Which means we'll still have to be careful. But at least I will have a job."

My crab cakes came, but I could barely eat them. I had too much on my mind. What was I going to do about the contest? What was Paige going to do? How would they live? I hoped they had savings.

Over dessert I told my parents about my conversation with Carol.

"Tough choice," Dad said, forking the last bit of baked potato into his mouth. "What are you going to do? Is it really yours?"

"I wrote every note and all the lyrics," I said. "Legally it's totally mine. Totally."

"Would you have been able to do it without collaborating with Paige?"

"I didn't collaborate," I said. "Did I?"

Mom shook her head. "I don't know, Kate. Only you can make that decision."

We drove home laughing because, after all, as my mom had pointed out, there were some very good things going on. I had been recognized, no matter what! They said I had a strong voice. My dad had a job.

But . . . Paige's dad would not have a job in two weeks. Paige had not won the competition.

Or had she? I just didn't know.

I went to my room, got Muffin, and took her out to the backyard with me. She snuggled up against me like a fur muff and purred, the vibration and her softness warming me from the outside in.

I sat down near the cold fire pit and thought and prayed.

There was no guarantee that Paige had come in second. If I gave up the prize, I wouldn't necessarily be giving it up to her. What if one of the other three had come in second? It would all be for nothing. What good would *that* be?

I prayed, and another thought came to me. If I was going to give it up, it wouldn't be because I wanted Paige to have it, as much as I loved her. It would be because it was the right thing to do based on song writing. There was no guarantee who would win.

Lord, I cried out. *Help me! I am stuck. Jammed. Wedged between two impossible situations. If I claim it, I may always wonder if it was the honest thing to do. If I give it up, I can't bring gifts to the reservation for Christmas. Even though Dad is keeping his job, there is no extra money.*

I snuggled Muffin close to me to keep her warm and paced the backyard, kicking a few orphaned leaves while some last brown, mossy ones clung to the rocks they'd been plastered to. The grass was brown. The trees slept.

Through the steamy window I could see my dad hunched over his desk. Was he working on his sermon?

The Philippians passage my dad had preached on a few weeks ago, the one I'd read on the top of his page, came back to me. "'Let nothing be done through selfish ambition or conceit,'" I said to myself. "'But in lowliness of mind let each esteem others better than himself. Let each of you look out not only for his own interests, but also for the interests of others.'" Philippians 2:3–4. Why had that verse stuck with me over the past couple of weeks while some of the others had wandered through my heart and left as quietly as they'd come?

Kitty's bell jingled in the evening dusk. Paige had been so sweet to give it to me. And even *more* important, to give me the song. Could I be the kind of person I admired in Paige—who has it all and shares, no sweat? Or rather, *had* it all. She was going to be dealt a big blow.

God did tell me to enter this contest. However, He didn't say I'd win. But I had won. Hadn't I?

I sat there for a while, shivering. The moon came out and rested on my shoulder. *God's spotlight,* I thought.

The only spotlight you need, I felt in my heart. My heart sank. I knew that voice.

God, if I give it up, there's no promise Paige will even win. Someone else might win.

That's not why you're giving it up. It's about you and me. Not Paige. But it's your choice.

What about Katie and the kids? Their presents. What about snobby Mrs. Doyle? You're actually going to let her win by not letting me give the gifts to the kids or by making me ask her for money?

I walked back into the house. "Do you want us to start a movie?" Dad asked. "Make it something special, since I don't get to watch movies with you two very often."

"I'm going to my room for a minute," I answered. "Yes to the movie. How about ... how about *The Passion of the Christ?*"

Dad nodded. I still didn't know what to do.

I put Muffin on her bed and looked out at the moonlight again.

I'm trustworthy. I heard it again. *Trust me.*

Then, what should I do? I asked the Lord in my heart. I waited again. Nothing.

Why hadn't I heard back?

CHAPTER ELEVEN
lewiston, idaho

paige

Why hadn't I heard back?

It was Wednesday. They'd said they would call on Tuesday. I was really, really tempted to call them. But I didn't. I knew that wouldn't look good, no matter what the outcome was.

Yearbook was cancelled *again*—Miss Jones's allergies had flared up. Youth group was cancelled, too, because a guest speaker was using the room. So I had nothing to do but wait for the call.

Janie breezed into the house and got on the phone immediately. I made faces at her, but she just turned her back to me. Mom was at a Football Boosters meeting, and Justin was at football practice. Dad, of course, was busy keeping the farms of the west wet at Rainmaker!

Mental note to self—be interested in others. Ask Justin how the season is going. Ask Mom how her day was. Ask Dad what is going on at work. He hadn't said anything for a long while.

Janie ran downstairs, covering the phone mouthpiece with her hand. "Call Waiting ID came on while I was talking. I think it's for you."

My hand was shaking. I knew who it was before I even asked.

"This is Paige Winsome," I said.

"Hello, Miss Winsome. This is Carol calling with Worship Works. I'm calling to tell you that you won the contest!"

I let it sink in. "Are you sure?" I asked.

"Oh yes," she said. "To be honest, when we narrowed it down after the first auditions, the five of you were pretty much equal. Between the first and second auditions, though, two of you really sharpened several key skills."

I couldn't stop the tears from coming.

"You, in particular," Carol went on, "seemed to

develop your voice more strongly. Did you have a voice coach?"

Voice coach? "Well, my friend gave me a few ideas," I said. "I don't know about coaching. She was a great help." I kept calm, on the outside. But inside I was screaming, *I WON!!!!!*

"Well, whatever you did, it really showed. It took your lead skills up a notch. Will you be ready to sing at half time next Thursday at the Turkey Bowl?"

"Will I!" I said.

"I'll give you a call later in the week with details on how long your performance must be and what time to arrive for sound check. Please email us with the correct spelling of your name as you'd like it to appear in the program announcement."

"I will. Thank you," I said. I hung up the phone. Janie looked like a lizard; she hadn't flinched a bit.

"Did you get it?" she asked. I think she already knew by my face.

"I did!" I said. "I really won!"

We jumped up and down and hugged. Then Janie reacted exactly as I knew she would.

"You need new clothes," she said. "Let's go to the mall. I have just the outfit in mind. Trust me, you're going to love it."

So that's how we went to the mall together on a Wednesday with no one except the two of us. None of Janie's glam friends. She hadn't been told she'd better take me or she'd lose her car privileges. She just wanted to take me!

We chatted on the way, but while my mouth was on one track my brain was on the other. Did I suddenly appear on her radar screen because I now had meaning in her world? Wasn't I okay just as plain ol' Paige before? I didn't know. I didn't want to fog the mood by asking right now.

And then there was the other thought. *Kate*. I'd think about it when I got home, I promised myself.

We rattled into the small mall near our home. "I wish we had time to go to Seattle for clothes," Janie said.

"It's only the high school," I said.

"You'll be up in front of everyone! Everything counts!" Janie pulled me into the mall.

I hadn't really given that much thought. What if I messed up? Would "Follow Me" be ready in time? I so badly had wanted for the world to see that I had value by being up there and letting them all hear me sing and play for once. It could all go the other way if I messed up. I could see Britt in my mind's eye, pointing it out to everyone. She knew just enough music to be dangerous. She could spot the mistakes.

"What are we going to pay for this with?" I asked.

Janie stopped. "Well, I know Mom would want to buy you something. I could call her on the cell phone."

"No. I want to tell her in person that I won."

"Well, we can spend a little. I have some cash, and Mom will pay me back." Jane snapped her Doublemint. "Do you have some good pants?"

"Cargo pants."

She shook her head. "How about some cords?"

I shook my head. "Not me."

"Jeans?"

"I have some new jeans that are good. And my new black boots."

She snapped her fingers. "Then the black sweater I have in mind will work."

We went to the sweater department and she clicked through several hangers before finding the style and size she had in mind.

"Voilà!"

I looked at it. I had to admit, it was very cool. No animal fur. But really soft. "I like it. How did you know it was here?"

"Constant window shopping sometimes pays off."

I laughed. "That sounds like it should be inside a fortune cookie."

I took it into the fitting room. I put it on, sucked my stomach in, and pulled my shoulders back. I looked at least sixteen.

"I'll take it," I said. "But how much is it?"

She looked at the price tag. "It's okay. But probably no more."

"There's something else I really want. In the accessories department."

"New earrings?"

I shook my head. "Nope. Come with me." I should be getting my allowance right after Thanksgiving. I knew just what I wanted to spend some of it on.

I wanted Ficcare hair sticks. I had seen them before, under the glass. Twenty-three dollars a pair.

"Look." I pointed out a pair under the glass. Glossy black, perfectly formed. Handmade, with a tiny real crystal in the tip of each stick. Not enough to be showy, but enough to catch the light.

"Cool," Janie said. "I haven't noticed you wearing two sticks before, though. New fashion?"

"Not two for me. One for me. One for Kate."

"Ah," she nodded. "Are you and Kate still going to be friends now that this thing is over?"

"Yes! We're really, really good friends. Forever kind of friends."

Janie nodded slowly. "How is Kate going to feel about this, you winning and all?"

The saleslady nodded to us. She was helping a customer and signaling she'd be right there.

"She'll be fine with it. If she couldn't win, I know she'd want me to."

"Well, duh," Janie said. "The real point is the 'if she couldn't win' part."

I said nothing and just waited there for the sales-clerk. I hadn't told Janie—or anyone—what Carol had said about my voice coaching. It was true that Kate had helped me with singing, and it showed. Carol even said so. I knew it. Kate knew it.

Would she regret helping me when she found out that I won? Would our friendship really last this?

As great as it was that those animals and the elderly people would have one another for companions, it was equally sad that Kate couldn't go and visit Kyle. Oh, I knew she could go and not do the Christmas program. Or rig up some lame dollar store gifts. But I also knew she wouldn't do that. She'd feel it was shaming to her and to them. Her heart and pride would both be wounded. Mine would have been.

"I'd like one set," I said to the clerk. She went to get a small black velour pouch to carry them in.

"Janie," I whispered, "if you pay for it now, I will pay you back after Thanksgiving when I get my allowance."

She nodded and paid for the sweater and the hair sticks. Then we headed toward the door. I saw the furniture store down the way.

"Can we stop by there?" I asked.

"Yeah. Why?"

"I want to look at beds. I'm sick of my tiny, ugly one. I'm thinking of asking for a new wrought-iron bed for Christmas."

Janie looked distressed. "Paige, they're expensive."

"I know," I said. "But we always get one huge present for Christmas each year."

Last year we each got new computers. A bed couldn't be more than that, could it? "Since when are you worried about money, anyway?" I tugged her arm this time, down the hall. "I'll buy you a pretzel. Come on."

We went to get a pretzel—mine with salt, hers with cheese dip—and then walked past the beds.

There it was. My dream bed. It was a wrought-iron daybed with a trundle—okay, like Janie's, but much prettier. It had intricate scrolls and dips and fleurs-de-lis all over. They looked like floral notes to me.

"There it is," I said. "It's perfect. And when Kate sleeps over, we can pull the bottom bed out and she'll have her own bed."

One reason I hadn't had Kate sleep over is that there was no place except the floor for her to sleep.

"Let's go," Janie muttered.

"What's up? I—"

"Let it go," she said. Then she brightened. "Let's tell Mom and Dad your good news. It'll cheer everything up."

I looked at her. Why did anyone need cheering

up? I didn't ask, though, since I didn't want my good day spoiled.

We drove home, but my parents were in the den with the door closed. I could hear Justin's raised voice. Oh great. I thought he was over that. He'd had an angry period with my dad last year, but this year had been so mellow. I didn't hear my dad yell back, though, so that was good.

Was his bad temper always going to spoil my good days? I steamed upstairs and logged on to the Internet.

A message from Walter. "Hey, Paige, any word yet? We're hoping for a big celebration night at youth group next week."

I felt a slow smile spread across my face. I would enjoy that. Especially now that Hayley came to youth group, too.

I emailed back: "I WON!"

My fingers stuck to the keyboard, though. My heart stuck to my ribs. I thought I knew why. "I'll call you later. Thanks for emailing!"

I looked at the pieces of paper tacked to the bulletin board above my computer. One was the fortune from the Chinese restaurant—before I even knew about the contest. The fortune said, "Big changes are coming." Now that the changes were happening, I wasn't so sure if they meant as much as I had imagined. Stability, please! I'd handled about all of the changes I could take.

There was a picture of Maddie and me in sixth grade, arm in arm. There was the slip of paper from Jake.

Jake! I'd email him next.

And there was a picture of Kate and me that my mom had taken at the Chinese restaurant after the final audition. My mom must have pinned that to the board yesterday when she was cleaning.

I took Jake's email address down from the bulletin board. My heart thumped, and I tucked my hair behind my ears. As if he could see me!

"Dear Jake," I wrote. Wait. "Dear" was too, um, glommy. I backspaced. "Jake." Much better. More direct. "It's Paige. Remember me? You showed me to Sunday school last week. Anyway, thanks for praying. God must be listening to you! I won! I'm going to perform at the Turkey Bowl. Please tell everyone else in the prayer group thanks, too. I hope to see you again sometime." How to sign off? I wish I could copy Kate and write "Chordially." It was so cool. But it was Kate's thing.

"Notefully yours?" Cheese. "In tune with you?" Double cheese.

I sat there. Finally I signed just plain, "Paige." I hoped he'd email back.

It was time to call Kate. I closed my door so no

one would come in and sank down on my carpet.

Lord, what can I say? In my heart, and in my head, I know Kate is the better singer. Maybe my song writing put me over the edge? Lord, should I turn it down?

I'd thought I wanted this all along, and now I didn't know. I had promised those pets to those people, and I realized now that was wrong to do when I didn't have the money in hand. *God, please forgive me.* Now I really didn't know how to say no—and I had a nagging feeling that I hadn't done the right thing all along. *When I started this, God, I had hopes. I wanted my family to love and see me. Now they do—I think—or do they just see the "successful" Paige? I can't stop thinking about Kate and all of her hopes. I wanted a friend, and now I have one who totally likes me for who I am. What if our friendship is over?*

I felt that strange warmth in my heart again. I knew I had to call Kate, and this was God's way of placing His hands over mine while I did the hard thing, just like He did when we composed music together.

I picked up the phone, half hoping someone would be on it. No one was. I called Clarkston.

"Hello, is Kate there?"

"Just a moment," her mom said. Her mom hadn't said hello to me. Was she mad at me, too?

"Hello?"

"Hi, Kate, it's Paige."

"Oh, hi!" I heard happiness but also hesitation in her voice. After all, she knew by now that she had lost, but she didn't know that I had won. I thought I'd make some small talk in case she wanted to ask rather than have me blurt it out.

"How is school going?"

"Good. I'm really busy right now though. How about you?"

"Yeah, me too. I put a lot of projects aside to work on the music. I have to catch up."

"Right," she said.

She didn't take my opener about the music to ask the question. I would try again.

"How are things with your parents? Your dad's job?"

Silence. Uh-oh.

"Both his jobs are fine," Kate said. She rushed on. "Did you hear from Worship Works?"

"Yes," I said. "I won."

"Congratulations," she said. "I am so glad. Really. I was wondering who would win."

That was a strange way to put it. She also seemed, well, calm. Not sad, really. But not happy. Maybe she was like my aunt Sue. Sue always said she needed time to "change gears."

"The lady told me that two of us rose right to the top," I said. "I'm sure it was you and me. I think it was your help with my singing that did it. I hope I was a good help to you, too."

"Oh, you were," Kate said. She sounded cheerier this time. "What are you going to sing at half time? I can't wait to hear it!"

"I'm not sure yet," I said. I decided I might as well go all out and say the whole thing. "Kate, I'm sorry you didn't win. If the truth be told, I think you're a better singer than I am. I'm not sure why I won, but I'm looking for ways to see what God wants me to do with it."

"I understand. You're a great musician," Kate said softly.

"Will this change our friendship?" I asked.

"No," Kate said. Then dead silent air.

But we both knew that we wouldn't know for certain till we saw each other in person. We needed time to think it through, to see what this meant. Maybe we were only meant to be short-term acquaintances and not long-term friends. I just didn't know.

"I'd better go," Kate said. "I am so swamped with work now at the end of the quarter, trying to finish before the Thanksgiving grade period."

"Me too," I said. She needed some time and space. I could see that. I just didn't want her to disappear. "I'll see you at the Thankgiving Day game though, right?"

"I'll be there," she said.

"Thanks for everything, Kate," I said. "I'll see you then."

I clicked the phone off. There was nothing to do but wait and pray. If our friendship was true, she'd be there. If not, it would be better to know.

I knew what song I'd sing, though. To honor God. To honor Kate, who had worked with the song in her own way. I opened my computer file and clicked on "Follow Me." It would take several long nights to get it done, and I sure hoped I wouldn't mess it up in front of thousands of people.

I looked at the black sack of Ficcare chopsticks on my dresser. I wouldn't wear them, or any chopstick, till the game. I'd only wear one if Kate came. If not, I'd return them and get my money back.

Please help me do this one last thing, Lord, I prayed. *This time it's not for me. It's for you.*

CHAPTER TWELVE
clarkston, washington

kate

Please help me do this one last thing, Lord, I prayed. *This time it's not for me. It's for you.*

It was Thursday night, a week before Thanksgiving, just before I'd slipped into sleep. But the days before that had not been so peaceful.

I'd thought that after I'd made the decision to let go about losing the contest I would be fine. And I was. After I called Carol, I had prayed that Paige would win. And she did. It was just so hard to hear it on the phone. The final blow was knowing that my help with her singing pushed her over the top and that was okay, but that her helping me with writing was not. Those were the rules, but they weren't fair. I didn't know how to handle it.

Last night at youth group everyone had been quiet and thoughtful toward me. People said, "I'm sorry," and I didn't know what to do with it. I found myself hating that they had to feel bad for me. I was used to being on top in at least *one* area, singing. It just reminded me of how poor most people in our church were, how poor my family was, and that I was always going to be in the section of society that someone felt sorry for. I asked Vickie to lead worship. I just couldn't do it with a pure heart.

I went home and cried my eyes out. Muffin curled up next to me and slept in my bed all night.

Kyle had emailed and asked how things went. Today, Thursday, I couldn't ignore him anymore. It wasn't nice. I emailed back and poured my heart out to him.

"I lost," I wrote.

Well, here's the whole truth, and I can only tell you because I don't want it to ever get back to my friend Paige because it would steal her joy. She gave me one of her best new songs to model my music after. I wrote my own song— lyrics and words—but I did use her model. When

they called to tell me I won, the contest coordi-
nator mentioned not getting any help. I wasn't
sure what qualified and what didn't, and so I
declined. The good news is, my friend Paige
won. The bad news is, I lost. I am so sad. Katie
and the kids at your church won't get good pres-
ents this year unless I can figure out something
else. I can probably mass order necklaces or
small stuffed animals. I just don't know. I'm so
sorry, and I hope you're not mad, although I
wouldn't blame you if you were. I am really mad
at God. Thanks for listening.

Kate

I clicked Send and sent it off. Then I went into the
kitchen to clean out the refrigerator and arrange the cup-
boards. My mom came out of her room wearing one of
the sweaters Mrs. Doyle had handed down to her last
year. It was like sticking a flame to the wick.

"What are you doing?" she asked.

"Distracting myself," I answered.

"Is your homework done?"

I nodded, chewing my gum for all it was worth. Snapping it. The sound felt angry, and I relished that.

"Do you want a friend to come over this weekend?"

I shook my head.

"Are you mad at Paige?"

I sighed and sat on the floor. "I'm mad at Paige. I'm

mad at me. I'm mad at God. I'm mad at Mrs. Doyle. I'm mad at you and Dad. I just don't know what to do."

Mom sat on the floor next to me and put her arm around me.

"Are you going to the game next Thursday?"

"I told Paige I would," I said.

"That's not an answer."

"I know."

I stood up and went into my room and got my guitar out. Yeah, right. Yet another reminder of the Doyles and everyone like them. I couldn't stand it, though. I had to play.

I strummed a few chords of my new song. All of a sudden I stopped and remembered the name of the song. "His Goodness."

Tears streamed down my face, and I set the guitar down again.

I logged on to the computer. Kyle was a guy, so he probably didn't read his email all the time—I didn't expect a response from him yet. Maybe there'd be something there from Paige. If she emailed me, I could probably email back.

There *was* an email from Kyle. I opened it.

Why are you mad at God? Did He promise you the presents if you declined Mrs. Doyle's offer? Come anyway. We'll have fun. We don't need presents. You and I didn't have them every year. These guys will be okay, too. I'm praying for you.

> *Kyle*

I sat in the dark of my room and finally laid my head down on my pillow and slept. I slept through the rest of the afternoon and dinner. When my dad came home, late, he woke me up.

"Hey, Sleeping Beauty," he said. "Come out and talk with Mom and me."

I walked out into the living room, feeling dizzy and disoriented. I'd gone to sleep in the afternoon and now the day was gone. I think my bones and my heart and my soul had been tired, and my body and mind had needed to be restrung.

"I'm hungry," I said.

My mom came out of the kitchen with three sandwiches—one of them a cheese with mayo and relish on white bread.

"Thanks." I took it from her and bit in.

"Do you feel any better?" Dad asked. "Mom said you were pretty much mad at everyone in the world."

"Now I can add one more person to the list," I said. "Kyle."

"Kyle?"

"Yes. For having the nerve to tell me the truth." I could see they didn't understand. I explained about the emails today.

"When I prayed about this contest, I felt like God *told* me to enter," I said. "If I am wrong on this one, how do I know I'm not wrong on everything else I think I hear Him say?"

"I see," Dad said. "That's a tough one. Could it be that you really *did* hear Him say to enter?"

"Yes, but look where it got me."

"As far as I see, it got you new insight into writing music and a wonderful new friend."

"A rich new friend." I sighed. I felt stupid as soon as I said it.

"This all comes back to money, doesn't it?" Dad said.

I nodded. "Look at people who have plenty, like the Doyles." I purposely avoided mentioning Paige's family, knowing her dad was almost out of work.

Mom called me on it. "Like Paige's family, who will be out of work soon?"

"I just don't want to be poor."

"We're not poor. If we had more money, we'd live in a bigger house in a different neighborhood. Most people in our church wouldn't relate to us nor we to them. How would we minister to them?"

"We still could." I kinda knew that might not be exactly true. I couldn't really see Paige's dad in our church. Or my dad preaching in theirs. Or Kyle's dad.

"We could. But the Lord calls each of us to someplace and to the work He's prepared for us to do. I wouldn't want to be Mark Winsome and have to answer to so many people about making money all day. I wouldn't want a job where I had all those worries to distract me from the flock God handed me. You have to remember who is responsible for my keeping my job."

"I know. God." I sniffed and melted some. It did make sense.

"God, ultimately, but Paige's dad worked hard to find a good buyer for the company and therefore saved my job."

I hadn't thought about that. Suddenly I felt a little happier that Paige had won. When I allowed that to lighten my heart, I remembered all the wonderful things she'd done for me along the way. Helping me with Muffin. Lending me her sweater. Giving me her song.

I was glad I had given her a ride to the first audition. I was glad I had showed her how to baby-sit better. I was glad that I had made the decision to step aside and let her have one big day to shine.

"He's even provided for us through the Doyles."

Now I really sniffed, but not because I was melting. "Maybe I should write a note to her and thank her for everything and then she might decide to send money to the Nez Perce reservation for the Christmas program."

"You can surely write a note to her," Mom said. "Thanking her for your guitar, if you mean it. But you can't do it with a hidden agenda in your heart."

"I still want the gifts for the kids," I said quietly. "Should I give that up?"

"Maybe you should ask God if He does. Are you will-ing to visit the kids if He says no to the Wee Care pres-ents?"

I nodded. "Yes. But I can ask Him, right? Is that okay?"

My parents hugged me. "It's always okay. We will pray for you that you get the gifts, too. You just never know."

I turned to go to bed.

"Kate," my dad called after me.

"Yes?"

"Are you going to talk with Paige?"

I shook my head. "I'm afraid I'll spill the secret about her dad's job. I told her that I had a lot of work to do but I'd see her at the game. She'll understand."

My mom came into my room and kissed me good-night.

"I don't like Anita Doyle, either," she whispered. "But there are rude people everywhere, inside and outside the church. I'm not going to let it change who I am."

I smiled and kissed my mom back. It was almost mid-night, and I couldn't sleep. I think Paige and I both knew that our friendship had really started only because of this contest. I'd read once that friendships start out of con-veniences—like you're in the same class or at the same church or on the same team. The true test of a friendship is if you stay together and grow closer after that conve-nience is gone. In seven days Paige and I would see if we had been growing a true friendship after all.

Cold moonlight streamed into my room, making Muffin's fur snowy white. I shivered under the covers.

"I'm sorry," I told God. "I assumed you'd do what I wanted. I decided what should happen, and then I blamed you when you didn't just fill my order like some kind of waiter. I wasn't worshiping you at all, and this was all about worship. Like the song says, I'm sorry, Lord, for the thing I've made it. It's all about you."

Peace and warmth tucked me in. "God, I would really like for those kids to have gifts. To shine. To celebrate your birthday with style and for them to reach their community with a great program. Please help me do this one last thing, Lord," I prayed. "This time it's not for me. It's for you. Is that okay?"

I felt that peace again. But this time I was listening rather than talking.

Before I fell asleep, I knew that over the weekend I would write a note to Mrs. Doyle and give it to her at church.

On Friday I came home from school and went over to the house of the people who had given Muffin to me.

"Hello. I'm trying to raise money for a mission trip over Christmas," I said. "Would you have any work for me to do to help you move?"

"Maybe," the dad said. He didn't seem as nice as the mom. I was glad I had Muffin now and he didn't.

I spent the afternoon and evening boxing up their garage. I didn't go home until about eight o'clock that evening. When I was done, he gave me twenty dollars. Twenty dollars after all those hours of work! I was covered with dust, and my arms ached. I wanted a bath and bed.

"Thank you," I said. I tried really hard to hold back the tears on the way home. I gritted my teeth.

Then I remembered. It was God who was to do the work, not me. "Thank you for this money, Lord," I said. "If you still want the gifts for the kids, please help me raise the money. If not, please let me know so I'm not making another mistake striking out on my own without thinking."

When I got home, there was an email from Paige.

"You okay? Hoping everything is going well with school. I know you're busy, so I didn't want to call. I'm still hoping to see you on Thanksgiving. I'm praying for your Dad's job situation—and mine!"

I didn't trust myself to start emailing because I'd either have to tell her the truth or avoid the topic, which might seem weird. I didn't want any more weirdness between us. Instead, I logged onto the Worship Works site and sent her a free e-card instead. "Miss you. See you on Thanksgiving."

I wondered if she'd find out about her dad's job loss before then and, if so, if it would affect her performance. I guessed they were still trying to keep it a secret till after the game.

Saturday I went over to the twins' house. "Do you need a baby-sitter this week?" I asked hopefully. "Or this month?"

Their mom shook her head. "If I did, I'd call you in a snap. But we've got to save some money for Christmas, so I'm trying to cut back expenses."

I tried to smile. I understood. I wrestled with the kids and made some spider shadows using a flashlight on the wall; then I went home.

Saturday night I emailed Kyle back.

"Thanks for what you said the other day," I wrote. "You're right. I know I told God what He was supposed to do, and He did what He wanted. Imagine that." I felt ashamed. Then I added, "I'm writing a note to a lady who supports our church tonight."

I sat there, fingers idling. I knew the reason I was telling him that was because I wanted him to like me.

He does like me, I thought. *I don't need to earn it*. I erased that line. As soon as I did, I remembered the part in the Bible about letting your good deeds be done in private and your heavenly Father would reward you in private.

Did I want Mrs. Doyle's approval? I closed my eyes and let the Holy Spirit search my heart.

No. Not anymore. I only wanted to be right with God.

I finished writing to Kyle and signed it, "Love, Kate." I sent it, even though I was blushing. Well, Christians are supposed to love one another, aren't they?

I clicked my overhead lamp on and took out one of my best pieces of stationery. Not too girlish, not too grown-up. Then I wrote the note.

> Dear Mrs. Doyle,
>
> I am sitting here with my guitar, and I just wanted to thank you for all of the nice things you've done for me this year. I hope I can do something nice for you sometime, too. Thanks again.
>
> In Christ,
> Kate

It didn't seem right to sign it "Chordially, Kate." She wouldn't get it. Besides, the reason I was writing was because we were in Christ together.

Saturday night I picked the movie. I chose *Miracle*. Of course.

The next morning I went to Sunday school and then went into the sanctuary and listened to my dad preach on Philippians again. He was so good. I looked at the clean November light pouring into our church and didn't want to be anywhere else. No offense against Paige and her big church, but I like small families, too.

Afterward I sought out Mrs. Doyle.

"This is for you," I said.

I don't know what I was expecting. I think I was expecting her to change, to smile, to hug me, to melt and have me see that when I did the right thing everyone else did, too.

Instead, she opened the note up and read it right there! She didn't even take it home to read in private! She licked her lips. Her lipstick was all worn off again, only lipliner remaining. She stuck the note back into the card.

"Thank you, Katherine," she said.

Katherine! Even my parents don't call me that.

"It's nice to have your hard work recognized by those you give to." I felt the door slam between us.

Then she turned and went to talk with someone else.

Used to be, I'd have balled my fists or spoken out. Now I knew it was all up to God. He changes, He provides. I had done my best with an open heart. I was willing to go to Kyle's church with little gifts—using all my money if I had to—and share myself with them, maybe singing instead. *Whatever you want,* I prayed. *It's out of my hands.* Instead of balled fists toward others, I had open palms toward Jesus.

We were always among the last people to leave, of course, along with our faithful friend Norm, who always stayed to help us clean up.

I went into the sanctuary by myself while my mom

washed out the coffeepots. I sat down with my guitar and played, softly. I didn't play my song. I just played what came to my fingers.

> *I know that my Redeemer lives;*
> *What comfort this sweet sentence gives!*
> *He lives, He lives, who once was dead;*
> *He lives, my ever living Head.*
> *He lives to grant me rich supply,*
> *He lives to guide me with His eye,*
> *He lives to comfort me when faint,*
> *He lives to hear my soul's complaint.*

I sat by myself in the church and let the tears cleanse my broken heart, and then He brought the peace that dried them. It was silent. No one else was in the room, but I heard it.

Well done, good and faithful servant.

I guess my next big test would be in four days. Thanksgiving.

CHAPTER THIRTEEN
clarkston, washington

paige

Thanksgiving.

The day was finally here. I woke up before anyone else, got out of bed, and shivered into the bathroom. Even Justin wasn't up yet. Last night I had heard him throwing up in the bathroom. An hour later I'd tiptoed down to his room to see if he was okay.

"Nerves," he said. Today was a big day for

him, too. I sat next to him on his bed for a few minutes remembering when we'd been little kids and used to play hide-and-seek in this room. Now he had a girlfriend and was planning a college search of his own for next year.

"I feel sick, too," I said.

He ruffled my hair like he used to when he gave me noogies, only it was softer.

I had slipped back into my room, wondering if I'd simply overlooked the fact that he had lots of things going on. He wasn't overlooking me as much as trying to balance all of the balls he juggled in his own life.

I figured maybe he was sleeping in. I showered, and when the bathroom steamed up I wrote "Good Luck, Justin. You're going to do GREAT!" in the steam on the mirror. I hoped he'd see it when he came to shower.

I wrapped a bath sheet around myself and headed back to my room. My clothes were all laid out. Blue jeans, the good ones that fit just right. Black boots. My new black sweater. Tiny black pearl earrings, because my hair would be pulled back. I took the bag with the chopsticks in it in case Kate showed up.

Would she come? We had said all along that we were a team. But I knew that I would have been crushed if I had lost. What would I have done about the pet placement? I knew she was ashamed to show up to Kyle's place for Christmas without the money for gifts. I understood. I wondered if I could help her at all.

I blew my hair dry and pulled it into a tight ponytail. I could always twist it in the chopstick later. I wished I had some makeup to wear. Good grief. A little wouldn't hurt.

Janie came into my room. "You're going to do great," she said. "I'm going to help out at the booster booth and take Justin to school. I'll be right up front with all of my friends at half time. Okay?"

I nodded and hugged her. She was taking my mom's place at the booster booth so Mom could stay with me up front, where I had to wait for the half time show. Mom and Dad would get good seats for the game there, too.

"Janie?" I called out. She turned around. "Thanks for taking me to get the sweater."

"You look great, Bugaboo," she said.

She hadn't called me that since I was a little girl. It made me feel teary. I'd miss her next year when she went to college.

I went downstairs and opened my piano. After stretching my hands out and warming up on the scales, I played "Follow Me." The house was quiet. Brie was on the couch next to me, but my mom and dad were upstairs getting ready and Justin and Janie were already gone.

The warm November smell of roasting turkey already scented the air. I knew my mom had baked two pumpkin pies. I saw them on the counter. They were plain, not like the fancy whipped cream ones we always bought. I jiggled one of them, and it looked soft in the center. But my mom had made them herself. I felt proud of the changes she was making.

I wanted them to feel proud of me, too.

On my second time through the song, I sang along.

The words were true, too. I *could* feel Him everywhere. I *heard* His voice in the beautiful voice of my friend Kate; I *saw* His hand loving me in the cup of cherries and grapes my mom had served me before I knew whether I'd win or not.

"I'll follow you anywhere," I sang. At that point, I didn't realize what that would mean.

After I was warmed up I went upstairs. Dad was in the kitchen finishing his coffee. I wondered if he thought I would bomb. He'd been avoiding me for the past few days, it seemed. Or maybe he was just busy at work.

"Ready?" he asked. I nodded. We had to be there early for the sound check, and I'd have to make sure that the keyboard sounded okay. For the thousandth time I wished I already knew guitar well enough to play it today.

We drove across the bridge to Clarkston. Funny, I had hardly ever gone to Clarkston before this autumn, and now I was going all the time. Now that I knew Kate lived there, it seemed more special.

The high school parking lot already had quite a few cars in it. Booster clubs and cheerleaders had gone through and woven strips of ribbon in both schools' colors along the chain fences. Balloons nodded and shook in the wind. I pulled my jacket around me. "Please warm up," I prayed. It was harder to sing in the cold, and I couldn't very well keep my gloves on.

I scanned the area for Kate. I didn't see her, but I hadn't expected her to be early, either. She'd probably sit on the Clarkston side anyway.

"Hello, Miss Winsome." It was Carol from Worship Works. "We're so glad you're here. Thank you for uploading your song to me this week. It looks wonderful. I am so glad that God has given you a gift for sharing your faith in Him with others. Your pastor and youth group must be very proud."

I nodded. Wasn't worth getting into that.

I tried the keyboard. It was a high quality one from the high school's music department. They hooked me up with the microphone. I felt sick again.

When Kate got up in front of people, it didn't matter who was around. She just sang and barely noticed. I wasn't like that, and right now I was really nervous!

"Miss Winsome?" Carol spoke again and I realized I'd been daydreaming. "To whom shall we make out your check?"

"Um, to my dad, I guess." I didn't have a bank account yet, but Dad could write the check out to the shelter for me. She made it out to my dad and handed it to me. I put it into my pocket.

After we checked out the speakers, Dad and I went to our VIP seats and sat down on neon orange bun warmers. Otherwise the metal would give us freezer burn. Mom was in the booster booth—with a great seat. She'd signed up to work the booth months ago.

I doodled on my program.

"How are you feeling?" Dad asked.

"Okay," I said. "I'm thinking about the song. I'm thinking about the pets. I'm thinking about all those little kids that Kate promised Christmas presents to that won't get them."

"Well, speaking of Christmas presents, I have some good news for you. I thought I'd tell you some of it right before the game to cheer you up."

"Oh, cool!" I stopped scanning the crowd for Kate and looked at him.

"Janie told Mom and me about the bed you want for Christmas."

"Janie!" I said out loud.

"She was trying to help as we were, ah, discussing something else. I wanted to let you know—you can have it!"

"Are you sure?"

"I'm sure."

I threw my arms around him and hugged him.

We sat there together in silence. A team of tiny cheerleaders walked by, five- and six-year-olds, I thought, in their little matching costumes. They were from Lewiston. I didn't see any tiny cheerleaders from Clarkston. Maybe they'd come later. Or maybe there just wasn't enough money in their booster club.

Those little girls reminded me of the girls Kate wanted to buy gifts for.

I sighed. I wished I could do something for them. My winnings just wouldn't be enough for both of us.

Dad poured some more coffee out of his Thermos and looked at me. "What's the matter? Nerves?"

I shook my head. "I just keep thinking about Kate." The cold air pinched my cheeks. "She tried as hard as I did. She helped me so much. I wouldn't have won without her."

"You girls knew at least one of you wouldn't win."

I nodded. I looked at the girls. I thought about the bed. I thought about the ski verses.

"'All the believers were of one heart and mind, and they felt that what they owned was not their own; they shared everything they had.'"

"Dad, would you be upset if I didn't want a bed for Christmas?"

"I thought you did! You've always wanted one like Janie's. But, of course, if you want something else, you can have it. Whatever."

"Whatever?"

Dad nodded. "Within reason. What's on your mind?"

The teams walked out onto the field and started to warm up. The band played in the distance. The air was clean, and the sky was scrubbed by the bubbles of clouds that had just slipped away.

"I want you to pay for those pet placements for me for Christmas. The two that I signed up for with the shelter."

Dad looked puzzled. "Aren't you going to do that with your winnings?"

I drew the check out of my pocket. "I had them make it out to you so you could write the check for me. I still want you to write the check, but to somewhere different."

"Where?"

"Do you think Kate's dad can keep a secret?" I asked.

Dad smiled in a knowing way that I didn't totally understand. "I know he can."

I handed the check to him. "Give it to him and

tell him it's for the Wee Care Christmas program. I don't want Kate to know where it came from. She won't enjoy it if she knows I had to give something up. This way she won't know. My pets will be taken care of and so will her kids." Dad didn't answer, but I heard another answer, inside me.

Well done, good and faithful servant.

My dad pulled me close. I had never seen my dad close to tears before. I think he keeps a wall around his heart that keeps all pain out but sometimes keeps us out, too.

The first half of the game seemed to fly by, and Justin did great. I couldn't have been prouder of him.

"He's sure to be the star next year," I said to my dad. My dad nodded sadly. I thought that was weird.

No sign of Kate yet. I sighed. It was okay. I had done what was right for her. I walked down to the place where I would walk onto the field at half time. I brought my music case, and as I stood up and looked toward the crowd, I saw several signs go up. One had "Go Paige!" written in large script with a music note under it. I looked to see who was holding it. Walter was on one side and Hayley on the other. I had a feeling Walter and Hayley had a lot more in common than I'd guessed. Another sign said, "Sing it, sister!" I smiled. Janie.

Last but not least, I spotted someone with a bouquet

of Mylar balloons. A set of chopsticks was drawn on every one. Kate!

I waved wildly to her and motioned for her to come onto the field where I was preparing.

She did. "I'm sorry I'm late," she said. "The balloons weren't ready!"

I hugged her. "I'm so glad you're here. I thought maybe you were mad and didn't want to come."

"I wouldn't miss it for anything," she said.

I grabbed the set of chopsticks out of my purse and quickly twisted my ponytail up. Kate twisted her hair back. She put the chopstick in mine and I put one in hers.

"We're a team," she said. "A win for one is a win for both."

I noticed Carol standing there with her mouth open. "You two know each other?"

I nodded and started to explain. Kate just bustled her away before Carol could say any more. Strange! "I'll see you right afterward," Kate said.

The announcer introduced me, and I walked onto the stage set in the middle of the field. My keyboard was on. My family was here. I saw Mallory and Britt, too, but they looked at me once and then walked over to the hot chocolate stand. I guess they weren't as in awe of the center stage as I thought they'd be. I learned something—I didn't care.

I sang "Follow Me." I wobbled for the first line or

two, but then I disappeared into the song. God's hands were over mine, and I closed my eyes and let Him show me the way. When I was done, it was mostly silent, still, and then people burst out in applause.

I said thank-you and left the field. My parents met me at the edge. "You did a great job!" Mom said. "We're so proud of you."

"Thanks," I said, just grateful that I hadn't thrown up or blown it. "Thanks."

Kate handed the orange balloon bouquet to me.

"Kate," I said, "do you mind if I let them go?"

"No, of course not," she answered. "But why?"

"As an offering," I said. She understood. I unclasped my grip from everything I thought I needed to be whole and happy and let it float into the air toward God. Tiny little orbs of orange reached out into the sky and then disappeared.

After the game we drove home, joking and laughing and *hungry*! Thanksgiving dinner never tasted so good. I even made our family's butternut squash casserole. The turkey wasn't store bought *or* dried out. My dad kept the television off. We all had so much to be thankful for.

After dinner that night my dad came up to me. "Mom and I need to talk with you at the burn barrel. Come on out."

I was surprised. Usually we played family games

on Thanksgiving evening, and we kids gave one another a tiny gift of thanksgiving when we weren't so distracted by the other stuff usually going on at Christmas. I went into my room and got my shoes and jacket.

"Mom and I have some strong news," Dad said. He pulled a yard chair over toward the barrel for me. "I'm losing my job at Rainmaker."

"No, Dad!" I gasped, confused that it had been kept a secret. I don't know why I was surprised. We knew it might happen. I just hadn't heard anything else about it, so I thought he'd been able to find a buyer or something.

"I thought you would find a buyer."

"I did," Dad said. "In Walla Walla. They run things a bit differently, though, and are bringing in their own management team."

"I'm so, so sorry, Dad." I felt especially bad that I had asked my dad to pay for the pets. What should I do?

"What will we do?" I asked. "Can you get another job?"

"I have another job," Dad said. "In Walla Walla."

"What?" I looked at my mom. "We're moving?"

Dad nodded. The sparks crackled in the burn barrel, and the warmth spilled over the top like steam from a boiling pot.

"The same company that bought us offered me a

job in their corporate headquarters in Walla Walla. We'll move during Christmas break."

"They were so impressed with the job that Dad had done, they offered him an even better job. But we'll have to move," Mom said. She patted Dad's arm.

"What about Janie? Justin?" I asked. Now I understood. I remembered all of their comments. "They know already, don't they!"

Dad nodded. "We wanted to wait till after the game to tell you so that it wouldn't distract you. Janie can stay here and finish her last semester. Mrs. Kellie said she could live with her so she can graduate with her class. We'll have to sell the house right away so we can afford a new one."

I had already prepared myself to separate from Janie for college, but not next month.

"Justin?"

"He'll finish the football season. He's a great kid, and I'm sure he'll make many new friends."

I knew he had a girlfriend, and I also knew how hard he had worked for his position on the team.

"Me?" I asked.

"You'll make new friends, too. We can make sure that you get to visit with Kate once a month or so. Maybe spend a weekend every other month. Okay? After all, you'll live in the same state now."

I knew Mom was trying to make it hopeful. I

mean, what else could we do? We had to go where my dad had a job.

"I'm sorry," Dad said. "I know I let you down."

I stood up and hugged him. "I'm not sorry. You did your best and I'm proud of you." Inside I was thinking: *What about Kate? The shelter? My nice neighborhood?*

"Maybe you'll have a chance to sing with the youth group in the new church."

I stood up. "What church were you thinking of?"

"The one we visited. Did you enjoy it there?"

Jake! And the youth group seemed nice, too.

We chatted for another minute or two, and then Dad stood up. "I'm going into the house to drag out a game or two and tell the other two to get ready for the kids' gift exchange. You're not too old for that, are you?"

I shook my head. I had thought to buy something small for Janie and Justin one day when they were still at school and it had been just Mom and me out shopping. Had they thought to buy something for me in all this craziness?

I sat outside alone awhile longer. The moonlight poured down on me, and I sang quietly to God.

"Lord, I think I'm a harmonizer," I said to Him. The trees rustled. "I feel better in the moonlight rather than the spotlight. I like how my music sounds coming out of Kate's mouth rather than out of mine."

A peace settled over me again. "It's okay. I think I found what I was looking for." I looked over the yard at the house, where my family was getting ready to exchange our gifts. "I understand."

I let the burn barrel die down. I wouldn't feed it my song journals. After all, those would be used to feed others.

I walked into the house.

Janie always got to get her gifts first, of course. I gave her a GummyWears choker like Kate's. Justin gave her a wrench. "For what?" she asked.

"Your car."

She threw a pillow at him.

Justin, second oldest, went next. Janie gave him breath mints. He threw the pillow back at her. I gave him an industrial-sized bottle of gel.

"My turn!" I said.

Justin handed his to me. It was in a brown paper sack. I opened it. "A box of fortune cookies?"

He smiled. "I saw them at the Christian bookstore. They have Bible verses in them. I know how crazy you are for Chinese food."

I hugged him. How perfectly cool. "Thanks!" I cracked one open and read it.

Matthew 10:39. I'd have to run and look it up.

Janie handed hers over next. "Another brown paper bag?"

I reached in and found a small wrought-iron knob. "What is this?"

"It's from my bed. Well, your bed."

"You're giving your bed to me?"

She smiled. "I guess so. I don't want to redo Mrs. Kellie's house, after all." I knew she was trying to make light of things.

I hugged them both. "I love you. But I'm still going to whip you at games tonight."

Janie threw one of the dice at me. Life was back to normal again.

We moved into the new house on December 22. As soon as I got the computer plugged in, I logged onto my email. I knew what would be there.

From Kate . . .

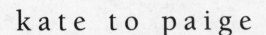

E-MAIL

kate to paige

So—how is the new house? Is it extremely cool? Have you had any company yet, of the boy persuasion? Ha ha ha.

Great news. You won't believe it. We got an anonymous donation with enough money for *all* the kids on the reservation—plus some extra for Lee and Nancy! I wish you could come with us, but I know how busy you are with moving and stuff. That was very cool for your parents to invite me to come and visit for New Year's Eve. I wouldn't miss it.

I don't even care if it *was* the Doyles after all who gave the money—I'm just glad it's here. I guess I'll be nicer to Mrs. Doyle now. Will you get to work for the animal shelter in Walla Walla? You'll have to show me all around.

Muffin is jumping up. 'spdtj]4w9u That was her pouncing on the keyboard.

What should I wear for the Christmas program? I want to look really good. For lots of reasons. Heh heh. Gotta go, my parents are starting the movie—tonight we're watching *It's a Wonderful Life*.

Love,
your best friend, Kate

E-MAIL

paige to kate

Okay, so we go to church yesterday and not only is JAKE there, but he says, hey, what are you doing here? I explain it to him, and he offers to give me guitar lessons at church before youth group if I show him stuff about composition. Is that cool or what? Woo-hoo!

The girls here are really nice, too. Except for

one. Maybe she's Britt's long-lost cousin. At least she doesn't sing.

Actually, I think I'd rather write than sing lead. You're a great singer. I know I'm not a lead singer. It's okay. I don't need that anymore. I like harmony. I'd rather listen to *you*!

I will totally help you think of something cool to wear. Maybe when I come to visit next week we can ask Janie to help, too. I know you admire her secretly. Don't deny it! I think she's okay, too.

All right, I'd better go. I can hear my mom calling. Email back soon.

> Love,
> your best friend, Paige

If your first concern is to look after yourself,
you'll never find yourself. But if you forget
about yourself and look to me,
you'll find both yourself and me.

Matthew 10:39 THE MESSAGE

Connect with other FRIENDS FOR A SEASON readers at *www.FriendsforaSeason.com*!

- Sign up for Sandra Byrd's newsletter
- Send e-cards to your friends
- Download FRIENDS FOR A SEASON wallpapers and icons
- Get a sneak peek at upcoming books in the series
- Learn more about the places and events featured in each book

www.FriendsforaSeason.com